Refurb - Text copyright © Emmy Ellis 2025
Cover Art by Emmy Ellis @ studioenp.com © 2025

All Rights Reserved

Refurb is a work of fiction. All characters, places, and events are from the author's imagination. Any resemblance to persons, living or dead, events or places is purely coincidental.

The author respectfully recognises the use of any and all trademarks.

With the exception of quotes used in reviews, this book may not be reproduced or used in whole or in part by any means existing without written permission from the author.

Warning: The unauthorised reproduction or distribution of this copyrighted work is illegal. No part of this book may be scanned, uploaded, or distributed via the Internet or any other means, electronic or print, without the author's written permission. The author does not give permission for any part of this book to be used in AI.

Published by Five Pyramids Press, Suite 1a 34 West Street,
Retford, England, DN22 6ES
ISBN: 9798292197416

REFURB

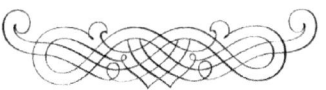

Emmy Ellis

Prologue

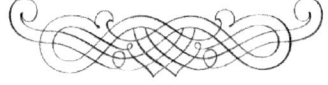

The switchover hadn't gone well. Getting stabbed hadn't been part of the bargain, although he'd been warned to always expect it in this game. His time in prison had taught him to be wary and watch people's hands to see whether they were going to come towards him, an improvised blade heading for the soft vulnerability of his body. But that was prison, and he hadn't expected it to happen in a street full of shops and people.

The buyer was supposed to hand over the money at the same time as he held the drugs out, both hidden beneath hands, thumbs holding the baggie and cash in place against their palms. The drugs had passed over before the money had touched his skin, and the man's other hand had quickly come up.

"Stop dealing or you'll have more than this coming your way."

And then the pain of a punch to the gut, the agony of something sharp withdrawing.

The buyer had run away with the money *and* the drugs.

Bewilderment. Incomprehension. Had this just happened?

He'd looked down.

Blood on his shirt.

People had stopped to stare, and someone was coming over, calling out and asking if he wanted help. No, he sodding didn't, not from the likes of a do-gooder busybody anyway.

Then he saw her in the window of the café over the road, another volley of shock to his system.

He'd wanted this yet had started to think it was never going to happen. He must have just got lucky, because before now he'd been wandering the streets aimlessly, hoping to catch sight of her. And now he had. But was it *really* her? She had different colour hair and had put on a lot of weight, but the eyes never changed, and he'd swear blind they belonged to her. Charlotte. The one he was convinced had sent him to prison.

The one he'd been looking for ever since he'd got out.

She caught him staring. Fuck, he wasn't happy about that. He didn't want her to know he'd recognised her. It'd been fine in the past when he'd been stalking her—until she'd twigged. It was supposed to be different this time, but once again, he'd fucked it up.

How much fucking up did he have to do before he got it into his thick head that it was time to pack it in?

He slapped a hand over his wound and ran, glancing over his shoulder to check whether Charlotte was still watching from the window, but instead he caught sight of a police officer getting out of a patrol car and chasing after him.

Jesus fucking wept, that was all he needed.

Chapter One

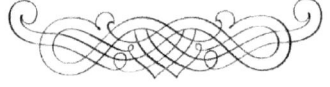

Sharon didn't need this, but it was okay, she was going to make out she didn't know who the stabbed man was. Two police officers had come into the café she ran for the twins. The Shiny Fork had a hidden space behind a wall out the back in one of the storerooms, stuff in there that likely shouldn't be there, so she was more worried about that being discovered than what had happened out the front.

How strange to be scared of the present when your past posed more of a threat. Or what you'd *done* in the past. The prison sentence and what she was doing were worlds apart—murder on one hand and hiding goods for the twins on the other. Although she wasn't the one doing the hiding, was she, it was them, and as she didn't own this café, then she did as she was told.

Having recently helped a Jamaican man by taking him to see the twins to get a gang brought down by the police, she thought karma had finally stopped paying her visits. She'd promised to be a good person, a nicer one, and helping Maven had been one hell of a big act on her part, considering she wasn't really Sharon Barker, and if the twins dug deep enough, they'd find out who she really was. Not that there was anything on record that would make her look too bad. She'd spoken to the police regarding an old lady sleeping in an attic, and that was literally what it would seem. They'd never find out the real darkness underneath it all, not from her.

The two policemen had finished speaking to the customers sitting at the tables closest to the window, and one turned to seek her out. She smiled at his approach, although in reality she'd prefer to give him a grimace. Every time she saw a police officer she shit herself inside while trying to maintain a calm outer appearance. It was much easier to come off as an innocent person when she had the kids with her. No one suspected mums, did they?

But the kids aren't here.

"PC Watkins. And your name is?"

"Sharon Barker."

"Did you see anything?"

"No, sorry."

"Not surprising if you were busy, I suppose. The customers haven't seen anything either."

She'd known that, she'd glanced around immediately after the stabbing to check. Everyone had been intent on their cuppas, food, and conversations. She hadn't given a fiddler's fuck that the man had been stabbed. He deserved it after what he'd done, and to be brutally honest, she hoped he died.

For the millionth time, she told herself off for thinking that way, paranoid that karma could actually read thoughts then act accordingly. It was so difficult to try and be good all the time, especially when people irritated her or the kids played up. She had bad thoughts then, too, but weren't they normal ones?

"Did you recognise either of the men involved?" Watkins asked.

"I've already said I didn't see anything."

"They've never come in here before?"

"Didn't you just hear what I said?" For all she knew, the stabbed man could have come in wearing a disguise. It probably wouldn't be the first time, because he'd stalked her before and she hadn't noticed for ages. Not until that horrible thing had—

"Thank you for your time." Watkins went to walk away and then paused. "Do you have any CCTV on the outside of your shop?"

"No, sorry. Dummy camera."

It wasn't, the twins had installed security back and front. People wouldn't necessarily want to rob a café, but they might want to rob what was behind that wall. Sharon had no idea what was in the taped-up cardboard boxes, but she suspected it wasn't bags of marshmallows. She was going to have to let George and Greg know that the police had been here—and that she'd lied about the CCTV.

The police left, and the chatter amongst the customers grew louder, a couple of them going outside, maybe to get a better view of any blood drips on the pavement over the road. People loved the macabre, although Sharon had experienced enough of that to last a lifetime and really didn't fancy any more, thank you very much, but now Mr Stabbed had spotted her, she could either wait for him to make contact or go and tell the twins.

But first she needed to hear from Seven, the one person who'd been by her side in the past. She'd sent their agreed text—Mayday!—not long after the stabbing, panic taking over a little bit because *he* had been out there. It could only mean one thing, that he'd found her and wanted to punish her for what she'd done.

She looked around and, satisfied the customers and staff were okay, she went out the back to her office so she could access the burner phone she used only to contact Seven. He had one, too. She'd checked hers every day for years, then once a week, then once a month, and had never imagined she'd have to use it. She'd convinced herself that changing her name would keep her safe, even though she'd known the possibility of that was unlikely. Plus *he* had been in prison, and she'd allowed herself to be cocooned by a false sense of security, her daily life overtaking any thoughts of the past.

Feeding the kids was more important than thinking about murder. Knowing her ex had cheated on her with a slimmer model, then set up home with her, was more important than worrying about the past misdemeanours, except the past really should have been her top priority at all times, but things changed when you got into a relationship and had children. The current life you led took over, and all its foibles and intricacies became your focus.

She locked the office door and sat at the desk to unlock the phone.

One message.

SEVEN: WHAT THE ACTUAL FUCK IS GOING ON?

She quickly tapped out: HE WAS OUTSIDE THE PLACE WHERE I WORK. HE GOT STABBED. LOOKED LIKE A DRUG DEAL GONE WRONG. NO SURPRISE THERE THEN, HE'S STILL THE SAME AS HE ALWAYS WAS. HE SAW ME WATCHING, SEEMED PISSED OFF I'D SPOTTED HIM. HE RAN OFF. POLICE CAME, BUT I MADE OUT I DIDN'T SEE ANYTHING AND THAT THERE'S NO CCTV. I JUST WANTED YOU TO KNOW

HE'S OUT AND OBVIOUSLY LOOKING FOR US, OTHERWISE HIM BEING HERE WAS A MASSIVE, MASSIVE COINCIDENCE.

She sent the message and went over to the Tassimo on the sideboard. George had insisted on having a coffee machine here that he could use whenever they popped by to go into the hidden storage area. She'd got used to them helping themselves, and it wasn't like she could tell them not to, considering this was their café, their goods, their profits. Everyone else who worked here basically ran the place, even though she was down as the manager. Her main role was to listen out for gossip and pass it on.

The phone bleeped.

SEVEN: WHAT ARE YOU GOING TO DO?

SHARON: I DON'T KNOW. I THOUGHT ABOUT TELLING THE TWINS, BUT I'M CURIOUS AS TO WHETHER HE'S GOING TO COME BACK, SHOW HIS HAND. HE'LL PROBABLY WANT TO ASK IF IT WAS ME WHO DOBBED HIM IN.

SEVEN: YOU HAVE TO PLEAD INNOCENCE.

SHARON: OF COURSE! WHAT DO YOU TAKE ME FOR? AND BEFORE YOU ASK, I WORK FOR THE TWINS, SO APPROACHING THEM ISN'T GOING TO BE AN ISSUE IF WE NEED OUR PROBLEM SOLVED.

SEVEN: I don't want anything to do with it. Keep my name out of it.

SHARON: So it's me carrying the brunt yet again. What a surprise…

SEVEN: I was on a steady keel until I got that message. I got myself sorted like you told me to. Got married, had two kids.

SHARON: I've got two as well, although the marriage part, I didn't get that far. He dipped his wick elsewhere. We split up ages ago now.

SEVEN: Sorry things didn't work out for you.

SHARON: Do you want to be kept updated or continue to bury your head in the sand? I remember you never did like me giving you any news on our situation.

SEVEN: Because I was depressed! Couldn't see any way out. But yes, with the kids and the missus to think about, I'm going to need to know if he's coming after me.

SHARON: Hopefully I'll be in touch with some good news.

SEVEN: Talk soon.

She plugged the burner into a power bank then popped it inside a locked drawer so no one saw it, intending to keep it switched on now that the ghost from their past had wafted back in. She fucking hated him so much. Why couldn't he have just learned his lesson by being imprisoned? Why did he always feel the need to control everything? Or did he have news for her, something she really needed to know? She was going to have to get brave if he approached her, letting him know in no uncertain terms that she had The Brothers behind her and this time he couldn't call the shots. Or he could but he'd have to face the consequences if George and Greg found out he'd hurt her, which was something he might do. He'd smacked her on the back of the head once.

She shoved the memory out of her mind, so hacked off that her life had changed in an instant. If she hadn't gone over to the window to clean the sill, she wouldn't have seen him, and he wouldn't have clocked her watching. She'd have been none the wiser, going about her day oblivious to the fact that she was being stalked again, so she supposed she ought to be grateful for small mercies. She'd had a warning of what was to come, and she could arm herself with the verbal weaponry she needed to tell him to piss off and leave her alone.

Back out in the café, she chatted to the customers and staff to try and take her mind off the turmoil currently playing out in her brain. She could get her ex to take the kids for the whole of this week instead of just his usual half, tell him she wasn't feeling too bright or something, but if she was being followed and watched, then they weren't safe whether they were with her *or* their father, because *he* could have followed them when they'd been collected from her flat. He could know exactly where to snatch them from if that was the route he was prepared to go down.

The afternoon dragged on, but the end of the workday arrived at last, all the staff gone after clean-up, the café smelling of the lemon-scented spray they used on the tables and counter. She drew the blinds, staring down at the two baskets on the windowsill, each filled with fake plastic goods—lemons and bread. She tried so hard to make this place somewhere people would want to be, creating a cosy, relaxed vibe, and it was always busy because the twins had used the same business model here as they had at their pubs: cheap prices, quality food.

She was going to miss this if she had to walk away. Again.

In the office, she collected her bag, popping both of her phones into it and zipping it up. She itched to have a cigarette—she only smoked when her anxiety spiked too high, and she congratulated herself on getting by without a fag when the stabbing had occurred. But after speaking to Seven and getting through the rest of the day on autopilot while her mind screamed at her that she probably had no more chances this time, her nerves were frayed to the point that one more brush against them would render them a tangled mess.

She might even end up like Seven had, depressed and staying in bed as much as possible.

No, she'd never go down that route. She hadn't last time and she wouldn't this time.

There was always the twins, she reminded herself. They had been really good to Maven, even after he'd admitted to belonging to a Jamaican gang that did terrible things. They'd allowed him to go home, alive, so if they'd done that for him then surely they'd do that for her? They knew her well now, too, although only the version of the tale she'd given them—that she was Sharon Barker, a woman with two kids, a saggy body, and an ex she'd begun to get along with for the sake of the children.

They didn't know the other side of her, and that meant she was going to have to reveal it. She couldn't expect them to help if they didn't have the full story. Maven had been brave and dished out the whole truth, even the ugliest bits, and the twins had gone into action, sorting it all out.

There was time enough for that if Sharon found she couldn't cope with this on her own.

She left via the back, setting the alarm, locking up, and stepping into the enclosed yard. She opened her bag, giving in and taking out her packet of Benson and Hedges. She lit a ciggie, the nicotine hit welcome but aggressive. Two more puffs was enough for her, so she chipped the fag and put it back in the packet—she wasn't about to waste it when they cost so much. She unlocked the gate using the longest key on the ring, closing it behind her, then relocking it. She dropped the keys in her bag, drew the zip, and set off along the pavement, glancing at the line of trees over the road that separated it from the playing field and a housing estate. She turned right into an alley, coming out opposite Superdrug.

She checked the area in case he'd come back. No one resembled him, so she crossed the road, entering Superdrug to buy the kids their daily vitamin gummies. She picked up some hairspray while she was at it, paid on the self-service till to avoid having to speak to anyone, then left the shop, looking left and right and all around just in case he'd come back whether he'd been stabbed or not. For all she knew it could have just been a surface graze. Blood always made it look worse than it was.

She walked up the high street, scanning the faces of everyone possible, anxious he was lurking in the crowd or he'd paid someone to watch her. Unnerved, she rushed to the end towards the taxi rank, getting into the first one in line.

She was going home, where she'd be alone, but better that than have the kids there, in danger.

Chapter Two

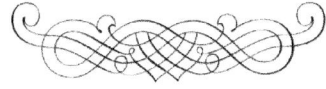

Charlotte supposed it would look a bit weird if anyone from 'out there' came inside and saw what was going on in the attic bedroom. This house wasn't exactly the type anyone would want to enter, though, considering Mint, a drug dealer, rented it out to desperate junkies. Charlotte wasn't desperate but she was hooked on drugs a little more than the average

user. Not necessarily a junkie. She didn't like that word, it made her feel well bad about herself. How she couldn't control the urges. How they controlled her. This must have been what Dad felt like when he was giving up smoking. He didn't want to do it anymore but couldn't stop the craving.

The old lady lying in the bed… She didn't belong here, she ought to be in one of those hospice places, but Mint was letting her stay here for a mate. They'd cooked up some plan together, where when the old bird died it'd look like she'd taken an overdose, but when she was going to die, Charlotte didn't know. She didn't want to know, couldn't stand the thought of being here when it happened, but what if Mint paid her to sit there while the breath ceased to inflate those ancient lungs? What then?

Fucking Mint. Such a tosser. He had everyone dancing to his tune, not only for their fix but the roof over their heads. Charlotte had been working on getting herself out of there, this rut, this world where she pretended she was fine, going to work, popping in to see her parents, when in reality she was a complete fuck-up reliant on the shit she sniffed up her nose. She'd get out of here, though. She'd run away with Seven, the bloke she'd made friends with. They'd start a new life, drug-free.

At one time she'd have snorted with laughter at that, drug-free, but people did it all the time, didn't they, got their acts together, and there was no reason, especially because they were so determined, that Charlotte and Seven couldn't do the same. If you had hope, then anything was possible.

Wasn't it?

She thought about what he'd told her, why he called himself Seven. He was the seventh child in a long procession of them and felt more like a number than a person. Sad, and one of the reasons he'd got addicted, she reckoned, to block out all the hurt of basically being ignored all his life.

An annoying ticking clock stood on the decrepit mantelpiece. Once upon a time it was probably quite grand, even if it was rumoured that servants lived up here all those years ago, but the plaster was crumbling on the edges, the lovely moulding chipped. Was it even plaster? Maybe it was stone. And what did it matter anyway? The clock itself it was in the shape of a Spanish pirate hat, and every time she saw it she imagined being on a ship. It was no surprise why. If she'd had a recent sniff along with her weed then of course she was going to be unsteady on her feet.

This whole house could do with a refurb—as could her life.

Sitting on the chair next to the sleeping old lady forced her to find things to do to entertain herself on the evenings when she forgot to bring her phone up with her and couldn't be bothered to go all the way down to the second floor, to her room, to collect it. That's when her mind wandered, back to the time when life had been pretty decent, no lies, no made-up perfection that she currently spouted to make people think she had it all together.

She'd told people she lived in a house with one of her old friends from school, Kerry, who was in on the subterfuge and had agreed to make out Charlotte rented one of her bedrooms that had an en suite. It helped for the times when Mum and Dad wanted to come round to see how she was. They saw a lovely posh house and didn't ask questions. If they nipped there while she wasn't in, Kerry made out she'd popped to the shop, then discreetly texted her to get her arse over there. Not good when Charlotte was high as a kite, and those times she responded with a text of her own that said she was too busy to come back. Kerry sent the parents away, and Charlotte dealt with the fallout later.

Everything was such a fucking mess. She was living a real-life version of a fake Facebook life, where everything was good and smiley and going well, where only the best side was revealed. Maybe people were envious of her supposed lifestyle, where she worked for a solicitor in her suits from Next and her high heels from Amazon. Where she had her hair done nice at the salon down the road; the truth was that she did it herself. The one thing she didn't do was her nails, she still kept up with the monthly acrylics, and to anyone looking at her, she'd seem absolutely normal.

How long that would last for was what had prompted Charlotte to try and get herself clean and save enough money to move out of this shithole. The four residents other than the old lady were in the same boat as her drugs wise, although she and Seven still successfully maintained the charade of living well, whereas the others had gone down the slippery slope that was so slippery that no matter how hard they tried to grab handholds on the mountain, they just kept sliding back down to the bottom. Totally addicted, spaced out a lot of the time, and pitiful to look at.

The old lady, Grace, sniffled. Charlotte turned to check on her. Oh, she was awake. What must it be like to lie there staring at the ceiling and not be able to move? According to Mint, the friend who Grace belonged to came by twice a day to inject something or other into her veins, evidenced by the bruising on the crooks of her arms. Also according to Mint, it wouldn't come as a shock to paramedics when her dead body was looked at because back in the day, Grace had been quite the heroin addict, and falling back into bad habits, even at eighty-two years old, could be believable, considering she'd not long become a widow, losing the love of her life.

"It's you again," Grace said, her voice croaky from where she'd been asleep for hours.

"Yes, it's me. What do you want to talk about tonight?"

"I need to get back to feed the budgie."

"I don't know about a budgie, and where is it you need to get back to?"

"My house."

"And where's that?"

"Five Prophet Gardens. If the nurses won't let me go home, will you go and feed the bird for me? His name's Pip. Lovely little thing."

Charlotte nodded, ashamed she'd allowed Grace to think she was in a hospice and that Charlotte was a volunteer who regularly came to visit patients. She'd been told to say this by Mint, and because it meant she received a couple of hundred a week for sitting there either chatting to Grace or listening to her steady breathing while she slept, it was money for old rope. And it wasn't like she could say no. Mint wasn't the type to take kindly to that word, and while she lived under his roof, she'd be better off doing as she was told.

"I'll go later if you like," Charlotte said, no clue whether the house was still Grace's or not. "How will I get in, though?"

"In the back garden, you'll find a summer house. There's an ornament of a budgie on the coffee table, and if you turn it upside down and slide the wooden base across, the key will be in there."

"Okay. Where's the budgie kept, and the food?"

"He's got a big cage in the living room, there's a sideboard next to it. The boxes of food are in there. Can you go now?"

"I've been told to sit with you until your nephew comes for a visit."

Mint's friend, although fuck knew what his name was and what he looked like. Charlotte had never bumped into him on the stairs yet, nor had she heard him going past her room on his way up to the attic. He existed because Mint said he existed, but he may as well be a ghost.

"I don't have a nephew…"

"Yes you do. He comes in the morning to give you your medicine and then again at night."

"How can I have a nephew if I don't have any brothers or sisters and my husband didn't have any either?"

Charlotte frowned. "Well, that's what I've been told he is. Do you not see him when he comes in?"

"I can't keep my eyes open for long anymore, so whoever it is, I wouldn't know they were here."

The thought of that gave Charlotte the creeps. Sleep was such a vulnerable thing, private, and the idea of this nephew person watching Grace when she wasn't aware of it seemed so wrong, but then wasn't that exactly what happened when Charlotte sat there? That didn't feel wrong, not in the sense that she was violating Grace's privacy, but it was very wrong that the old woman was here at all, especially because a drugs overdose was imminent.

Charlotte ought to be going to the police station and letting them know that an old lady was being held in an attic, thinking she was being cared for by nurses, when instead, murder was on the cards. But she didn't want to piss Mint off; to her shame, she still needed him for drugs and accommodation. Just until she'd weaned herself off the coke and saved enough money to move somewhere else. That's what she did with the money Mint gave her for these sitting sessions; she popped it in a pot that she hid up the chimney in her room where a couple of the bricks were missing, invisible to anyone else.

"So will you go? Now?" Grace asked.

"I'll have to find someone else to sit with you."

"I don't need anyone. I'm tired." Grace closed her eyes and turned her head slightly towards the wall beneath the window.

Charlotte stared at her. There was no way she could leave the old girl when she'd been paid to sit here, and besides, Mint could show up at any minute to check whether she was doing what he'd asked her to. So she leaned her elbows on her knees while Grace fell asleep to the tick-tick-tick of the Spanish-hat clock. Once Grace's breathing had evened out into deep inhales and exhales, Charlotte got up to retrieve the walking stick leaning against the fireplace. She tapped on the floor three times, paused for three seconds, then repeated the triple tap. Putting the walking stick back, she opened the door and leaned on the jamb, waiting.

The creak of Seven's door below had her thankful that he was awake and had heard her knocking. She stared at the banister rail and balusters, waiting for his head to pop into view on his way up the stairs, smiling at him in the dim light of the bare forty-watt bulb above him. The blond curls on one side of his head had matted where he must have been lying on his bed, probably watching telly, knowing him. His flushed cheeks indicated he'd not long taken a sniff, although he was doing really well and barely had much these days. Both of them bought the same amount as they used to from Mint so they didn't get accused of going elsewhere for it, but they sold on what they didn't use.

She stepped out onto the landing, closing the door behind her so Grace wouldn't overhear the conversation should she wake up.

Voice low, Charlotte said, "She's going on about a budgie called Pip and told me her address. And get this, she reckons she hasn't got a nephew, so what the fucking hell is going on?"

Seven frowned. "Mint must have lied to us, but then that isn't a surprise, considering there's plans for the old bird to die here. Why do you care what's going on anyway? It didn't bother you before when Mint asked you to look after her sometimes. You were more bothered about adding money to our escape fund."

She couldn't deny that. "But I didn't expect to feel sorry for her, did I? Back when I started sitting with her, I was still pretty fucked up on coke and taking a lot more than I am now. Maybe I've grown a conscience, God knows, but I said I'd feed the budgie."

"What? Why would you want to get more involved than you already are? Your fingerprints are in that

room as it is, but it can be explained away because you're going to make out to the police you sat in there with her, which is completely true, but how the hell would you explain your fingerprints in her house?"

"There won't be any. I'll wear gloves."

"But what if one of your hairs falls on the floor or something?"

"I can put my bobble hat on, and anyway, it's going to look like an overdose, right? So why would the police even need to go to her house if the death isn't suspicious?"

"Maybe they'll wonder why an old lady's in an attic, in a rented house with people she doesn't know. God, the amount of questions that could be asked…"

"I'm curious now as to whether she even has a house of her own. She told me where the key is to get in. Will you come with me? I've only got to sit here till ten, then Mint said I can go."

"I'm only going to come because I don't want you going on your own. It's worrying me that she said she hasn't got a nephew—because if not, who else is coming to see her? Maybe she's got dementia and she forgot."

Charlotte shrugged. "I don't know, but I'll see you downstairs about five past ten, all right?"

Seven sighed and stared at the ceiling. "All right."

Chapter Three

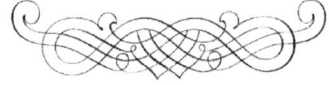

Since they had a lull, George and Greg had gone back to basics—cleaning up the scum from the streets, the entitled little twats who thought they had a right to swan round Cardigan doing whatever the fuck they wanted. Many of them had discovered it didn't work like that, and that the rumours about kneecappings and

Cheshire smiles were true. Only two smiles had been given, though, and both arseholes had been taken to the private clinic to get sewn up. Two people walking into an NHS hospital with slits from ear to ear meant questions were going to be asked. The same with the kneecappings, only two, but the other miscreants had been treated to a variety of punishments, all that could be attributed to random fights, drunken attacks, or some nutter going round hurting people for fun.

They currently drove around the Estate in their little white van. It always gave George the feeling of being in their early days again when they were out on the hunt in it, only it was different from the past because they had Ralph the dog with them, his head currently poking between the two front seats. He liked to watch where they were going. Ralph was usually with Martin during the week, accompanying him on his rounds to collect protection money, but he was off to the doctor's this afternoon about his chesty cough.

Ralph panted, his tongue hanging to one side.

"Do you need a drink, mate?" George asked. "Go and get one."

They had a special doggy water dispenser that had suction feet so it didn't move when the van was in motion. Ralph just had to lick the nozzle and it let a trickle of water out into a deep bowl. Ralph understood the command and disappeared into the back. Hopefully he'd have a drink and settle down on his bed.

Greg took one hand off the steering wheel and pointed at a man in a suit getting out of a fancy car and going to the boot. "What's he doing?"

"Park up."

Greg stopped at the kerb behind a blue Kia, arms folded. George watched the fella take a holdall out of the boot, close the lid, and then walk to a small green where kids were playing football, a couple of mums on benches nearby, one with a pushchair. The man placed the holdall under the pushchair, took a large envelope from one of the women, then strode back towards his car.

"That looked dodgy as fuck." George got out and crossed the street, standing by the man's driver's-side door so he couldn't get in that way.

"What's your fucking game?" Mr Holdall asked.

"What's yours?" George lowered his sunglasses for a second then put them back on.

"Yeah, it's me, so if you'd like to explain what you were doing…"

"Taking some washing over to my wife."

George laughed. "Do you think I'm fucking stupid? What's in that envelope?"

"Papers she signed."

"What papers?"

"To say who gets what. We split up last week." Mr Holdall opened the envelope, took a wedge of papers out, and handed them over.

George scanned them. He hated it when his suspicions were proved wrong. He gave them back. "Why did you give her some washing?"

"Because the machine broke yesterday and we've got a baby and a toddler. I did the washing for her this morning then gave it back."

"You've got a machine."

"Yes…"

"So why haven't you unplugged it and taken it around her gaff when it's clear she needs it more than you?"

"Because *I* need it…"

"How is she getting a new one?"

"I don't know."

George shook his head. "D'you know what, fuck off out of here. I'll deal with it." He stomped over the grass to the benches, lowered his sunglasses again so the women could see who he was, then asked, "Mind if I check that holdall?"

"Why? It's just got my kids' washing in it."

"I want to see."

"Go on then."

He took the holdall from beneath the buggy and undid the zip. Neatly folded baby grows, vests, and older children's clothing filled the bag. While it looked like it was innocent, it may well not be, so he did a thorough search between items. Finding nothing but washing, he put the bag back.

"Sorry about that, but we don't trust anybody. Who was that bloke?"

"My soon-to-be ex-husband."

"Why was he doing your washing?"

"Because my machine broke."

"Right, give me your address, and someone will be round your house within the hour with a new one."

Her eyes widened. "What do I have to do for it?"

"Fuck all."

She told him her address, and he typed it in his notes app, holding his hand up in a wave while walking away towards Greg who'd let Ralph out for a run on the grass. The dog chased a football the kids were kicking, the children wetting themselves with laughter when he chased them, too. George came to a stop and sent a message to Moody about the washing machine, then he slipped the phone in his pocket.

"What did you find out?" Greg asked.

"Nothing except the fact that the bloke's a massive penis. I'll tell you in the van in case one of these kids overhear us. I might swear."

They returned to the van, Ralph flopping onto his bed and groaning as if in complaint that they'd spoiled his fun. George told Greg the little story.

"Sounds like she's well shot of him," Greg said, "but at least he did the washing for her, which saved her the job."

"Fair enough, but it hadn't even entered his head to give her his machine or go and buy her another one."

"You should have marched him down to Currys instead of letting him go, forced him to buy one."

"Do you know when you're that pissed off with someone you can't even be bothered to do that? Well, that's where I was. It was easier and quicker to get the job done myself."

Greg pulled out of the parking spot, and they continued their perusal of the Estate. They stopped by some of the fronts they owned—hairdressing salons, pubs, a small corner shop—and ended up at the Plaza. George had a bag of baby things he'd been collecting for Ichabod and his missus, Marleigh, whose baby was due in a couple of months. He must nip to their new house and deliver it to the expectant mother.

They parked round the back of Jackpot Palace amongst the stolen cars that Dwayne had nicked ready to be sold on, entering the casino via the back door by inputting a code in the keypad.

They walked down the corridor until they came to Ichabod's office. George tapped on the door, and hearing the Irishman telling them to come in—he would have seen them on the CCTV monitor—George went in first and plonked himself down on a seat in front of the desk. Greg opted to lean against the wall by the door.

Ichabod looked well for not working out in the field anymore. He'd been training Moody to take his place in surveillance and beating the shit out of people, if necessary, although no one would be as good as Ichabod, in George's opinion.

"How are ye?" Ichabod asked.

"Not too bad, mate. You?"

"Doin' good. Marleigh had a scan the other day."

"Everything okay?"

"Yes, the wee one's growin' fine. He'll be playin' wid Rosie soon enough."

George smiled at the thought of Janine's little girl. "He will indeed. Thought of any names yet?"

"Still undecided. Anyway, I doubt very much ye came here tae talk about me and mine. Is there a problem?"

"Not here as far as we're aware, unless you're going to tell us different?"

"Everythin' is goin' along well enough."

"So there's no one we need to teach a lesson?"

"I did that myself. Took him out the back and gave him a good pastin'. Feckin' eejit thought it was okay tae steal someone else's chip off the table. Admittedly, when we looked at the CCTV afterwards, it seemed he was telling the truth—his finger did nudge the man's stack as he was collecting his own, and one of the chips had rolled across to him. Whether he saw that or not we couldn't tell."

"And you hit him anyway."

"Of course, just in case."

George laughed and stood. "We'll be off then."

"There is one thing you can do for me."

George paused and waited for Ichabod to elaborate.

"Since we moved from Marleigh's place tae one of our own, we've been havin' a bit of trouble wid the neighbour again."

"The one giving you gyp about the bins?"

Ichabod nodded. "Ye did say tae let ye know if my gentle persuasion wasn't workin'."

George opened the door. "It gives us something to do."

They left, getting in the van to Ralph acting as though they'd left him for ten hours instead of ten minutes. Greg drove off in the direction of Ichabod's place. Ralph scrambled between the seats, making a right mess of it with one of his paws going into Greg's groin, but he eventually landed on George's lap, whimpering, no doubt telling him in doggy language that he'd felt *so* abandoned and unloved.

"Pack it in, you dozy mutt."

George stroked him until they arrived at their destination. They left Ralph in the van again, although he watched them from the passenger seat, nose up at the partially open window. George caught sight of Marleigh in one of the bedroom windows, and he waved then gestured for her not to come down, that they weren't there for her. She soon gathered that when they strode down the neighbour's driveway.

An old man opened the door to George's heavy knock. He was as Ichabod had described, grizzled, a red nose from booze, crinkly hair, and a turkey neck.

"What?" the man barked.

"Mr Timmons?"

"Yes, what of it?"

"George and Greg Wilkes."

"What about it?"

"We heard about the bin issue."

"Ah good, because that Irish bastard next door doesn't leave his in the proper place when he pulls them out for collection. They're supposed to be against the kerb, not against his garden wall."

George glanced across at said wall which stood about half a metre high. "I don't understand why he can't put his bins there."

"Because it's the rules. The council says they have to go on the road against the kerb. That way they don't cause an obstruction, where *his* way, anyone with a buggy would have to steer around it, and anyone walking two abreast would have to go single file. It's the selfishness of the inconvenience it causes others that gets me, and you'd think with her having a bun in the oven that they'd be more considerate of the pushchairs. She'll be using one soon, and you can bet she'll change her tune then."

George had to admit the bloke had a point, but he wasn't going to say so. "I'll speak to the homeowners and ask them to please be respectful and put them at the kerb in future."

"You can do it now. She's at her window, look. One of those nosy types."

George apologised on Ichabod's behalf and moved on next door. He knocked and waited for Marleigh to answer. She let them in without him having to say a word, and George glanced back. Mr Timmons smirked as if he thought she was going to get in trouble. Door closed, they walked through to the big kitchen at the back. Marleigh lowered herself to a stool at the island, indicating to the fridge.

"Help yourself to a cold drink or make a coffee," she said. "My ankles are getting swollen now, and I'm really tired today."

"If you need Ichabod at home more, just say so." Greg took two cans of Coke out of the fridge and handed one to George, then closed the back door. "There are plenty of people to do his shift at the casino. And I take it you'd like a cup of tea."

"That would be lovely, thank you. I see you met with our lovely neighbour. Miserable old bastard. His son's just as bad."

"Who's that?"

"I heard the old boy calling him Minty."

George opened his can. "I thought this address was familiar when Ichabod said you'd moved here. The son is the same bloke our men had to have a word with about selling drugs, except we were told he was called Mint. So why is he just as bad?"

"He came round yesterday and had a go about the bins. I assume that's why you're here because Ichabod told you. He said he was going to ask you to deal with it because he didn't want to cause any fuss here."

"It's best not to shit on your own doorstep," George said, the sound of the kettle rumbling in the background. "So this Mint came here on his own, did he, or did he have mates with him?"

"On his own, and I suspect he waited until Ichabod had gone out."

"A coward, then."

"Hmm."

"What did he have to say?"

"He said he'd report us to the council if we didn't put the bins at the kerb next time."

"Do us a favour and do what he asked. The old fella made a fair point about it being an obstruction when you put them against your wall."

Marleigh sighed. "Okay. The politics of suburban life…"

"We'll have another chat with this Mint, even though one of our men gave him a little present of a stab wound yesterday as a warning."

"Ichabod mentioned drugs."

"Yep. Stay away from the pair of them next door, but keep your ears open and let us know of any developments. How did Mint seem to you when he came round?"

"He didn't look like he'd been stabbed, put it that way."

"Maybe the blade didn't go in deep enough. It was a bit of a tricky call, done in town, lots of people about, so it wasn't as if our man could stick around to see if he'd done the expected damage."

Greg brought her tea over and placed it on a coaster. They drank their Cokes in between chatting about the baby, which reminded George that he had a bag in the back of the van. He popped out to get it, Ralph telling him off for leaving him again.

"We'll be back in a sec, grumpy." He took the bag inside. "We won't stop to watch you unpack it, but if there's anything in there you don't want, feel free to take it down to the clinic for other mothers and babies."

"Thanks, you're very kind."

George nodded, and they said their goodbyes. Back in the van, George sent message to one of their men, telling them to meet Dwayne in half an hour at a specific location to collect a stolen car in order for surveillance to be done. He wanted the house next to Ichabod's watched—or specifically, Mint, and maybe Mr Timmons, too, the cantankerous old goat.

Chapter Four

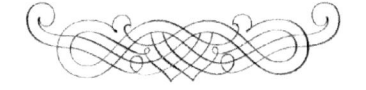

Sharon hadn't expected to get the message, but there it was, plain as day on the burner: I NEED TO SEE YOU. Her Mayday text to Seven must have unsettled him. Of course it bloody would have, she'd be the same in his shoes, but in her opinion, there wasn't any need for them to meet just yet.

They'd agreed it wasn't wise for them to see each other unless they absolutely had to.

It was the day after the stabbing, and nothing untoward had happened since, but then it wouldn't have, would it, if there had been a hospital visit and stitches involved. The nurses may have alerted the police about the stab wound, and *he* may have been spoken to, giving him no chance to turn up at her place. Did he even know where she lived?

For the first time since George had told her the flat was on the ground floor and she had a garden, she wished she was a few flights up. What had once been seen as a luxury was now a worry. Break-ins were so easy to do on the ground floor. The image of an open window flashed in her mind, and she shuddered, thinking about the window in her past and how someone had climbed through it to commit a crime. It usually happened that way, flickers of her past intruding when she saw something innocuous. To others, an open window meant letting in the breeze, but to her it could mean so much more.

She shirked off those seeds before they grew into unruly thoughts, something she'd battled with for years—thoughts meant you worried, got yourself coiled up, sometimes for absolutely no reason. Her anxiety had come from her relationship with cocaine, and it had remained while she'd been cutting down and trying to get off the gear, and afterwards, was at its worst when she'd lived in a flat with Seven. They'd intended to hide out, mind their own business, but it hadn't worked out that way. Seven had gone into a pit of depression where life didn't have much meaning anymore, whereas she'd gone in the opposite direction, her mind alive with scenarios, intrusive thoughts, and worries about the future.

She stared at the burner phone. Fucking hell.

SHARON: WHERE AND WHEN?

SEVEN: NOW, AT THE BACK OF THE CHIPPY.

That was going to be a blast from the past, going there. She hadn't been in that part of London in what felt like forever, and she'd promised herself she'd never go back. But here she was, sitting in her office at the café, contemplating it. Was it a stupid move? Yes, but she knew Seven, and if he didn't get some reassurance from her in person, then he was likely to spiral.

Sharon: Now isn't possible because I don't live there anymore. It's going to take me at least half an hour to get to you.

Seven: Okay. I'll wait.

Sharon: In a car or…?

Seven: I walked here.

So he'd still stayed in the area where they used to live, the stupid bastard, yet she'd gone to another Estate to make sure there was less chance of being spotted. She pushed up off the desk and went out into the café to let her staff know she was going out for the rest of the day. It wouldn't bother them, they were used to dealing with everything by themselves, including locking up.

She exited the back way, not wanting any spies out the front to see her leaving. She went left and rushed along the backs of the shops. At the end of the street, she stepped across the T-junction to head towards an alley between two of the houses that stood in a long row of many. A turn left out of the alley, and she was in Croftwell Street and waiting for a bus that would take her to the station, where she'd get another to one of her old haunts.

She didn't recognise him at all. Like her, he'd put on weight, and he'd grown a beard like he'd said he would. Weighing heavier suited him. The last time she'd seen him he'd been painfully thin to the point she'd worried he'd waste away. That was why she'd insisted he go with her to the chip shop a few nights a week, not only to get him out of hibernation mode but to ensure he ate. During that time he'd rarely left the flat other than to go to work or on the chippy walks.

It had all been so sad when she thought about it.

He stood beside the double wooden doors where a Transit with the chip shop logo on the side had backed up. It zipped her straight back to that night they'd come here when—

Seven peered over at her through sunglasses, raised a hand as though he wasn't sure it was her, then waved when he realised it actually was. She'd bet he hadn't expected her to get in such a state. She really had let herself go, and weighing heavier didn't suit *her* at all, the mirror told her that every time she looked at herself. It had been so easy to pile on the pounds—maybe it had been a form of depression after she'd had the children and the ex had cheated. Food was a comfort, but better that than cocaine. And she had to cut herself some slack. Years had passed since she'd been the slim young woman who'd taken her nice figure for granted, thinking she'd been fat back then when really she'd been skinny compared to now.

No amount of self-empowering memes about positive body image were going to make her love herself.

She walked closer to him, and he raised the sunglasses as if to reassure her, still from a distance, that it was him. It was so weird—it was Seven but not Seven, just like she was Charlotte but not Charlotte. But she felt like Charlotte again now that she was looking into his eyes. If he was anything like the old Seven, he'd expect her to take charge of this new situation so he didn't have to.

"Let's go and talk over by the trees," he said.

She hadn't been able to see them the last time she was here, it had been dark, but she understood why he'd want to talk away from any waggling ears; employees from the shops could come out at any second for a smoke.

They crossed the road that went along the back of the delivery yard behind the shops and walked over the grass. She shuddered at the point where they'd stood years ago, when everything had been so different.

At the tree line, she noted she'd been right before and that a wall ran behind the trunks. She stood between one of them and the wall, leaning her back against the bricks. He did the same a metre away.

A bird circled above the shops, probably waiting for someone to drop a chip.

"Why did you need to see me?" she asked, then made a joke: "I mean, it's not like you're looking at the same visual as before, is it?"

"You shouldn't put yourself down. My wife does that, and it isn't good for your self-esteem. If you don't love yourself, then how can you expect others to?"

"Oh God, you've become one of *those* people, have you?"

"I had to learn to give a toss about me when we parted ways because I didn't have you there anymore to lean on, so pardon me if I've become one of *those* people."

"You're talking as if it was my fault that everything happened."

"Some of it was, like when you phoned the police the first time."

"Don't tell me you still think it's okay that an old woman could have been murdered."

"No, I don't think it's okay, but it did a number on my mental health, you know that more than anyone, and…"

"And what? What do you want from me? I had to stay strong for both of us, and it was hard, and when we moved on it was a massive relief that I only had to look out for myself, where as you…you'd looked out for yourself the whole time."

"You can't kick this man while he's down anymore, Char."

"Don't call me that."

"Don't change the subject. I won't put up with you talking down to me like you used to. I understand why you had to because not a lot was computing for me back then, but I've done a lot of work on myself, and…God, it doesn't matter."

"You didn't answer my question. Why did you need to see me?"

"Because we're moving next week, it's been in the works for months, and I wanted to say goodbye."

"Where are you going?"

"Italy. For work."

"Nice. So did you stay around here then?"

"Yeah, switched my job to working from home. Kept my head right down, got the shopping delivered an' that. Barely saw anyone."

"So how did you meet your wife?"

"She was a colleague. How did you meet your…"

"He's an ex. Met him down the pub. I threw myself at him basically, to get through, to have someone looking after *me* for a change. It went wrong, and now I'm a single mum. No regrets, though."

He scuffed a foot over the grass. "You know you said you worked for the twins. Did you mean *the* twins?"

"Yes."

"How the fuck did that come about?"

"I had to help someone. Turned out he was in some really deep shit."

"Deeper than ours?"

"Equally as bad but in a different way."

"And you work for them now because…"

"They asked me to, simple as that."

They remained quiet for a while, Sharon staring at the tree bark.

"So the stabbing," he said. "It was definitely Mint?"

She hadn't thought of him by his name for ages. "He" or "him" made it easier, but she supposed now that he was in her life again, she may as well acknowledge who he was. "Yes, it was definitely him." She went through what had happened so Seven had a clearer picture.

"Do you think he'll be back?"

"Probably. He'll have questions, you know that."

He glanced at his watch. "I'd better go. I left my wife doing the last bits of packing. Like I said, I just wanted to say goodbye. And thanks. You know, for what you did. I wouldn't be here if it wasn't for you, but I think you know that already."

She had wondered how close he'd come to…yeah, to that, and she ought to be proud of herself, because even though she'd been pretty tough with him at times, her attempt at saving him had worked. Italy, eh? He'd never have believed it if someone had told him that's where he'd end up—she wouldn't either. She wanted to ask him if his wife knew about his past addiction or if he'd kept it a secret like she had with her ex, but what was the point? Maybe she was trying to prolong this meeting because he was the only friend she had left from her old life.

Maybe she was going to find it hard to properly let him go.

"I bumped into your mum the other day," he said—did he feel the same need to hang around? "She asked if I'd seen you. She asks that every time. It broke her, you leaving, just so you know."

He shoved off the wall and walked away, over the grass and across the road to the left which led to an alley. Eyes stinging and with a big lump of guilt sitting in her throat—because he could have said anything else to her but that—she went the other way, coming out down the side of the shops. She was going to test the water by going into the chippy and seeing if anyone recognised her. If, of course, the people from all those years ago still worked there. It had retained its name, but that didn't mean anything, did it, because people sold businesses all the time.

She pushed the door open, immediately assaulted by the smell of fish and chips, and cloying air that seemed to have oil particles clinging to it. It was gross, especially as it was hot outside. She stood in the queue with two other people, which gave her a chance to study the workers behind the counter.

The owner from back then stood cooking chips. He looked up, and they made eye contact, but he popped his head back down straight away, not because he'd recognised her but because he hadn't. She didn't bother buying anything. She walked out and went to the newsagent's. The same owner was still there, too, although he was well old now with his white hair and hollow cheeks. She picked up a packet of crisps to eat on the bus and went up to the counter.

"Bloody hell, Charlotte, long time no see. Your mum was only in the other day, and we were talking about you."

Her heart thumped faster. "I didn't know you knew each other."

"We didn't until you buggered off into your new life. We got talking that first time she was here because she was looking for answers, wanting to know why you needed some space.

She's been here every week since to check whether you've been in. Are you back?"

"No."

He scanned the crisps. "Will you be going to see her?"

"No, it's best I don't."

"For you or for her?"

She tapped her card on the reader. "For her and my dad."

"That sounds a bit ominous."

"It is when somebody could go after them because of me."

"Oh." He bit his bottom lip. "Should I warn them? I think I'd better do that."

"If no one's bothered them in all these years, then I doubt they will now, and if you tell them there's an issue then they're bound to go to the police, and then the person might hear about it and go round their house anyway. So basically, your big mouth could get them hurt." In her panic and irritation, she'd snapped at him when she hadn't meant to. Fucking hell, why did shopkeepers have to be so nosy?

"I see. So it's worse than we thought."

"Been having a good gossip about me, have you?"

His flushing cheeks said it all.

"*Don't* gossip," she said. "It's too dangerous, especially now the person in question is out of prison. Don't talk to anyone about me, especially the fact that I was here."

She flounced out of the shop, angry yet afraid at the same time that her parents might be dragged into this when she'd thought it had been put to bed. All because of her stupidity of going into the shop. If something happened to them now it would be her fault.

Chapter Five

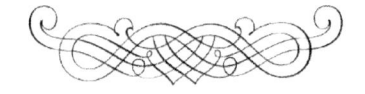

Prophet Gardens wasn't what Charlotte had expected, all posh with well-kept gardens and windows that gleamed from the nearby streetlights. Expensive cars sat on driveways, two vehicles on a few of them, and there was an air of 'you don't belong here' which set her on edge. She could still play the part, though, of someone who belonged. She never allowed

herself to look a state in public, a little voice in the back of her head always telling her she had to keep her chin up and appear respectable. She looked respectable now in her Lycra running gear, her nice trainers, and a long puffy coat, all in black. Oh, and a bobble hat and gloves.

The walk here had been a bit awkward to be honest. Before they'd even left home, Seven had made it perfectly clear he didn't want to go on this mission, despite saying he didn't want her to go alone, so it had confused her. And he didn't want to engage in conversation. Maybe he'd had a bad day at work. Or maybe he was happy about her putting money into their escape fund but he didn't want to actually do anything to contribute to it. After all, for some reason, Mint had only approached Charlotte to sit with Grace.

They stood beneath the overhanging oak tree branches on a slice of grass between two of the homes where they'd approached from the street behind. Charlotte stuffed her hands in her coat pockets and peered across the circular central green that all the houses surrounded. She imagined everybody gathered there for barbecues in the summer and wished she'd never left that kind of life to enter the one she currently lived. Mum and Dad's street often had gatherings, tables set up in a line on the road, and Charlotte had been so exhausted by it all that she'd craved something completely different. Funny how, now she'd had something completely different, she wanted to go back to how it had been.

Her breath puffed out in clouds—it was bloody cold this winter, and Christmas wasn't far away. She was tempted to stamp her feet to get some warmth into them, but she reckoned Seven would give her a filthy look because the thudding would draw attention to them. One of the only things he'd said on the way here was that they should get in the house, feed the bloody bird, give it a bit of water, and leave.

"Shall we go over there then?" she whispered.

He nodded. "I mean it, in and out." He paused. "If it's even her house. Like I said, dementia."

They stepped out from between the houses and walked on the pavement rather than go over the green. Just two people out on a stroll, nothing to see here. Still, it felt like they were doing something wrong, even though Grace had given Charlotte permission to find the key and enter her house. But what if that permission was given because Grace thought the house was still hers? And if it wasn't, how the fuck were they going to explain themselves if they got caught? But if it was Grace's, what if the so-called nephew was in there? Okay, there weren't any lights on, but he could be asleep, couldn't he?

Before indecision and worry could force Charlotte to run back the way they'd come, she walked faster and led the way down the side of the house into an alley bordered by six-foot-high fencing both sides. She tried the handle of the tall gate to number five, and it turned. She went into the garden. In the light of a security lamp that snapped on, which took her aback for a second, she spotted the summer house straight away, bottom left, a little pond in front of it with a tinkling fountain that sounded loud in the quiet of the night. She glanced over her shoulder to check that Seven was coming with her and, at his nod, she moved out of the way so he could also come into the garden.

A patio slab path bisected the grass and paved the way to the summer house door. Seven shut the gate and followed her. Charlotte pushed down the handle of the door and went inside, surprised the summer house didn't get locked when there were things inside that could be stolen. There was enough light that she could see: the coffee table Grace had mentioned sat in the middle on a polished wooden floor, a sofa stood against the rear wall, and to one side on the right, an armchair with a side table next to it. On it, a silver photo frame.

Charlotte moved closer, her nosiness getting the better of her.

In the photograph, Grace stood next to a man, the pair of them smiling wide, their eyes seeming to sparkle. Grace had to be at least thirty years younger, so in her fifties, and she looked so elegant and put together, so different from the old woman Charlotte knew and the one described to her by Mint of a desperate druggie who'd do anything for heroin. The photo didn't convince Charlotte that Grace had been down on her luck, but it would have been taken after all the convoluted mess that heroin would have brought to the woman's life. She'd have had time to dry herself out, pick herself up, and dress in the type of clothes that made her look respectable.

Just like Charlotte did.

It was all a charade, living. You spent half the time pretending to be something you weren't, wishing you were really that something you were projecting, instead of accepting who you actually were.

It was exhausting.

She snatched her gaze away from a smiling and happy Grace to the bird ornament on the table. Double-checking she had her gloves on, even though she knew she did, she reached out and picked up the bird, sliding the bottom panel away and finding the promised key.

As she put the panel back and replaced the bird, they were plunged into darkness with the security light going off.

"Should we wait for a bit just in case any neighbours look out of the window and see us in here?" she asked. "I mean, that light is going to snap on again, so…"

"Just for a minute or two."

Seven turned towards the house; no doubt he'd be interested in the ones either side, too, to see if anybody was watching. Charlotte clutched the key, waiting for him to tell her they'd been spotted and they'd have to make a run for it, but he didn't.

Instead, he said, "What will you do if we go in there and there's shit we can sell?"

She couldn't say she hadn't thought the same herself. A few trinkets here and there, stuff easily put inside a pocket, but could she stand to sit with Grace again if she'd stolen her belongings?

You're sitting with her knowing she's going to be killed, so what's the difference?

Charlotte shrugged at herself; there was no difference, and getting as much money as possible to move out of Mint's was the only goal she should be concentrating on. "Maybe there will be, then you can steal it and flog it—and finally put some decent money in the pot."

"I wondered when you were going to do that, make a dig. I told you from the beginning I can't put much in the fund. You've seen my finances, you know damn well I don't have anything much to spare."

That was true, and he tapped his mum up for money to buy drugs. She had a fair few quid knocking around and handed it out as though it was nothing, just to get him out of her house or her face. That was his excuse for taking drugs in the first place, to block out the fact that Mummy dearest didn't love him like she should. Charlotte felt sorry for him, he'd had it bloody rough, but if he wasn't prepared to go to therapy, which was free with his work health package, then she didn't want to hear him whinging about it.

"What about the money you get from selling the drugs you buy from Mint? We agreed whatever we made it would go in the pot, but so far I haven't seen you hand over any."

"I've been having to pay my mum back. She said she wouldn't lend it me otherwise."

That sounded a bit too convenient, but Charlotte wasn't going to get into it now. She'd had the forethought to get a notebook that they both signed whenever they put money by. When they got a new *place, she'd have saved ninety percent of the deposit, and she was going to let him know that he could pay her a bit extra every month to cover his portion. Why should she pay it all? It wasn't like they were lovers or anything, just two people thrust together because of living in the same house and taking the same drugs and having the same landlord.*

Their friendship, it was a weird one, but it was the only one she had in this, her real world, the only person who knew exactly who she'd been when she was at her worst. There was a bond that formed between people who'd shown their most vulnerable side, who'd been so fucked off their faces that they hadn't even known the vulnerability had come spilling out of their mouths, words that couldn't be remembered afterwards, tears that had dried, leaving the skin tight and the eyes sore.

There was a link that couldn't be broken—even if they went their separate ways, it would always be there. She couldn't work out yet whether that was good or bad.

"Come on," he whispered. "Let's get this done."

Seven stepped out of the summer house, mugged by the brightness of the security light, raising his hand to shield his eyes—or maybe he was trying to hide his face, just in case. Charlotte supposed that was sensible, and she did the same as she followed him out. She shut the door and trailed him up the garden, coming to a stop at some patio doors. She took the key out of her pocket and had a look quickly before the light snapped off again. It wasn't the type of key for a front door, which was a relief, because she'd been dreading entering that way, people seeing them. It was more like it belonged to the patio doors, small and silver, so she slid it into the lock and twisted. A soft clunk denoted she'd been successful, and, mindful of how loud patio doors could sound when they were slid across, especially late at night, she pushed it slowly until there was a big enough gap for them to go inside. Seven went in with her, and she closed the door when the security light blacked out.

She drew the curtains then took her phone out of her pocket to use the torch. She flashed it around to get her bearings. They were in a dining room, the table set for two people, which was odd. Crockery, cutlery, wine glasses, water glasses, napkins, all there as though it were a restaurant. Was this how some people lived? Were they that posh? Or had Grace been about to have a meal with someone when the 'nephew' had turned up to collect her, taking her to Mint's attic room?

Charlotte shivered and felt a bit guilty now that she was actually in the woman's home. She had to be disturbed in the head if she thought it was okay for

Mint's friend to overdose an old lady. She remembered the evening Mint had told her about it, three or so months ago, and Charlotte had been off her tits, her mind hazy, the giggles never far away. She'd told herself the next morning that what he'd said was something her mind had conjured up while she was high, but he'd said the same thing again the next night, and again the first evening she'd gone up to the attic to find Grace in bed.

I am not a nice person.

But she could be. She could help Grace by going to the police.

"Should we tell on Mint?" she asked, inspecting a bowl on top of a plate. It had a layer of dust on it.

"We've talked about this before," Seven whispered. "If we tell the police then we get ourselves in the shit, too. You've gone too far in this to be able to back out and look innocent."

"All I've done is sit with her and talk to her. I could make out I didn't know about the murder from the start, just that I was told this evening or something."

"Why, are you getting uncomfortable now you're standing in her house and seeing that she's an actual human being who had a life before she was stuffed up in the attic?"

Him putting it like that made Charlotte feel a bit sick. An old lady 'stuffed up in the attic'. God, it sounded so fucking awful—because it was!

"Shit," *she muttered,* "let's feed this sodding bird and get out of here."

"So you're not going to look around for some stuff to nick?"

"I don't know. Don't put pressure on me. I'm all confused as to where I stand on this now." *She could murder a proper fat line of sniff, her go-to when life got tough, but she gritted her teeth and walked through a doorway to get her mind off temptation. Not that she had any coke on her, nor in her room, but she knew exactly where to get it, and that was the problem.*

Maybe Mint ought to die instead of Grace. That would solve things.

She kept that thought to herself.

In a hallway with three doors either side, Charlotte was about to open one in an attempt to find the living room when she remembered her earlier thought: the pretend nephew could be asleep upstairs. She pointed to the ceiling to convey to Seven what she intended to do. He nodded and gestured with a finger that he'd check the rooms down here.

Charlotte walked upstairs, holding her breath the whole way in case one of the steps creaked. Luck was on her side, they remained silent, and she continued on to the landing, opening the first door. It revealed a spacious bathroom with a claw-foot tub and one whole corner devoted to a shower area. It was the stuff made of dreams, and a pang of envy twisted in her gut. She'd had so many dreams when she was younger and she'd still yet to own a bathroom like this.

Instead of wallowing on her shortcomings and drug-taking that had prevented her from getting what she'd wanted, she tried all the other doors, getting more and more antsy with each one, worrying that at some point someone was going to jump out at her. But every room lay empty, and in what she guessed was the master, she used the torch to see the top of the furniture, and again, dust had settled, enough that it matched the amount of time that Grace had been in the attic.

Why was the nephew taking so long before he killed her? Did he want it to look like she'd had a psychotic break and had run to Mint's house, and he was busy all this time trying to find her, the good relative that he was? And why would Mint be prepared to pretend he'd rented a room to an old lady, when he could be implicated in her death by any one of the other residents informing the police that he was not only their landlord but a drug dealer? It didn't make sense, unless **he** *was the pretend nephew and he'd made up a story that some other bloke was.*

She moved over to a vanity table, spying a jewellery box that was similar to a briefcase but smaller. She put her phone down so she could press the little lock buttons and open the lid. Jewellery lay against a backing of black velvet: chunky bracelets with fat gems; rings; earrings. If these weren't paste, then they were likely worth a lot of money.

Before she could change her mind, she grabbed it all and stuffed in her coat pocket. She sensed that horrible feeling coming back where overwhelm was about to take over. Guilt, too.

She couldn't stand it here any longer. She had to get back downstairs, find the birdseed, put a load in a bowl for Pip, refill the water, and get back out into the fresh air. It was musty in here where the house had been shut up.

She went back downstairs and found Seven in the living room by the window, one of the open curtains hiding him from view outside.

"Turn that bloody torch off," he said and beckoned for her to join him.

Charlotte slid her phone in her pocket. She went over there and looked out, too, frowning at a car parking on the other side of the green. The headlights went out, but nobody left the vehicle. It could be a resident who didn't want to go indoors yet, some bloke who was sick of his wife and kids, or a mother just taking five minutes before she walked into the nuthouse again. But what if it was something to do with this house? What if the person in the car was going to sit there and spy on it?

Why the hell would they, though?

She pushed those stupid thoughts out of her head and said, "You keep an eye on what's going on over there while I find the birdseed."

"There's no point."

"What do you mean, there's no point?"

"The bird's dead. It's gone fucking rotten in the bottom of the cage."

Charlotte felt sick. "Bloody Nora." She glanced around to see if she could find the cage. There was enough light from a streetlamp for her to see it in the corner. She moved closer, squinting in the gloom, and yes, the bird was dead, on its back with its skeletal claws sticking up in the air. "We need to leave."

"I was just going to say the same, because someone's got out of that car and he's coming over the green."

A quick inhale from shock dried her throat out, and Charlotte swallowed to wet it, darting across the room to stand with Seven. Mint came stomping over in his signature black donkey jacket, jeans, and combat boots, his hair slicked back, all nice as usual, and she swore she could smell his aftershave. Mint wasn't the type of drug dealer who looked like one. Anyone would think he had a good job way up the ladder. Maybe that was how he planned to get himself extricated from any blame regarding Grace's murder. He could say he was just a landlord and had no idea what the residents got up to. And as for them accusing him of being their dealer—would they really? No. Charlotte thought back to how she'd been at her most desperate, her most hooked, and there was no way she'd have told anybody who handed her the powder. She wouldn't have wanted him to stop giving it to her, so his identity would have remained a secret.

Now, though? Was she prepared to grass him up to the police now that she'd stolen a shitload of jewellery from Grace's little box? Once it was sold she'd have more than enough to keep her going, to get the fuck out of Mint's den of…of whatever.

He came closer, opening the garden gate as though he had no cares about being seen. Maybe he didn't. Maybe he had a right to be here and he just wasn't saying. The more Charlotte thought about it, the more obvious it was that he was going to kill Grace and blame it on some nephew or other who didn't even exist.

How could he pull that off when there was no nephew? Grace herself had said so. But then Seven had said about dementia. Oh, fucking hell, this was all getting a bit much.

Mint walked up the garden path. Charlotte remained frozen next to Seven. What if Mint had a key? What if he came in here and caught them? Why the hell hadn't they fucking legged it out the back as soon as they knew it was him getting out of the car?

"Oh God," Charlotte said.

The knock on the door startled her; she hadn't been expecting it at all.

"Why is he bloody knocking when he knows Grace isn't here?" she whispered.

"How do I know? Be quiet."

She stood there with her heart thudding too loudly, her chest going tight where she was teetering on the verge of a panic attack. In order to stop it, she had to be proactive, but if she got on her hands and knees and went into the hallway, he might see her shape through the glass in the front door. She hadn't taken any notice whether it was plain or patterned and couldn't take the risk. So she breathed deeply, eyes closed, then opened them again when Seven nudged her.

Mint was walking back over the green.

They waited for him to drive away, Charlotte puzzling over why he'd come here and what the real truth was. Then they left the house via the rear, hoods up, heads bent. Charlotte had her hands in her pockets, holding the jewels with one and her phone in the other. If she told Seven what she'd stolen then he'd want to claim half, even if that wasn't fair because she'd done the nicking, and once again that would mean she'd put another chunk in the pot and he hadn't.

No, she was going to keep this to herself.

They didn't talk on the way back. What was there to say other than Pip was dead, clearly left to starve, the dining table was set for two people, and Mint had turned up for whatever reason. Did he know about the jewellery box, was that it? Was he checking to see if anyone was in and he'd come back later to do some thieving?

Probably. He was a devious bastard like that.

Chapter Six

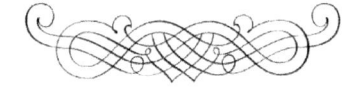

Mint hadn't expected to move in with Mr Timmons after he'd got out of the nick, but his wife, who'd be an ex soon, had commandeered the family home as hers. Before he'd gone to prison, he'd only been living in it for somewhere to doss anyway; their relationship had hit the rocks way before he'd started seeing other people behind her back.

Mr Timmons was his dad, but he'd only ever known him as the bloke who ran the little shop at the end of the street where Mint had grown up. All his life he'd thought he didn't have a dad, that he'd run off to join the army and had never come home, yet every day he'd seen Timmons and Timmons had seen him.

He couldn't bring himself to call the man Dad just yet, although it might not be long before he did, seeing as Timmons was doing a bang-up job of being a father. Now. Mint was going to have to have a word with his mother about why she'd never revealed who his dad was, but ever since he'd walked out of the prison gates, he'd avoided going to her house. She'd written to him while he was inside, but he hadn't responded.

Timmons had applied for a visiting order and explained things, saying he was getting on a bit and it was about time Mint knew about him. Forty-eight years after his birth. That was a lot of ground to cover, but they'd get there eventually.

So now it was back to business. It had been bloody difficult trying to find a supplier after the last one had cut him off — and who could blame the bloke. Mint had owed him money, and the drugs had been swiped by the pigs when they'd arrested him.

That's why Mint now lived on the Cardigan Estate. There was no way he could go back to where he was before. While he'd been away he'd employed a trusted mate to collect the rents on the three Victorian houses he owned. When he thought about it, with the drugs included, he'd had quite the empire going. Still did, really, except with the drugs he was starting from the ground up again. Going round pubs and touting for business. Swapping drugs for money on the streets instead of at his houses. He'd been imprisoned for so long that many of the addicted tenants he'd once known had moved on, new people in their places, and his mate had done bloody well in getting all the rooms painted and whatnot. He'd basically turned them into decent accommodation for decent people rather than a scabhole for scabs.

Because of that, Mint was coining it in more than previously on the rents, even with his mate taking a cut for a cash-in-hand wage. To be honest, he was glad to be leaving that part of his life behind. Chasing druggies for rent hadn't been fun, although threatening them when he'd sold them drugs was.

He glanced at the time. Eight in the morning. He winced at a tugging in his side from the stab wound stitches. Thankfully the blade had only been a couple of inches long, and the nurse friend of his who'd patched him up had suggested co-codamol for the pain. She'd given him a prescription for antibiotics, saying she'd put it on his record that he'd come into A&E with a tooth abscess.

He didn't know who those Brothers thought they were, sending someone out to shiv him like that—now he'd had time to think about it, he realised it had to be them behind it. A trick, obviously, setting it up like a drug sale, when all along the fucking bastards had sent a warning.

"Stop dealing or you'll have more than this coming your way."

It was all right, he'd learn to be a bit more circumspect, to duck and dive. He'd soon know the lay of the land on this Estate, who to trust and who not to. Give him another year and hopefully he'd be back at the top. It took time to get suppliers to trust dealers, he couldn't expect everything to be hunky-dory straight off the bat.

He tried stretching out on the sofa in the living room, but it pulled his stitches too much, so he returned to the foetal position. Timmons was out there making him a cuppa and a sandwich, trying to be a good dad. Mint was going to be a good son—on the outside at least. Timmons had told him all the money he'd received from the sale of his shop was in a trust that he could have when Timmons had died. It had echoes of the past to it, the leaving of money, an elderly person's death, and it gave him the creeps a bit. Not so much that he wouldn't take the cash when the time came, though.

He was well aware that some would say he was a bastard with how he'd behaved, and how he continued to behave, but some people just didn't have good genes, did they, despite their parents being okay. Mint rarely had a conscience, even when it came to his kids. He hadn't wanted them, Ashley had tricked him into it as far as he was concerned, saying she was on the pill when so she so clearly wasn't.

He reckoned people would tell him that he ought to take more notice of his kids, considering how he'd felt as a boy without a dad, but a lack of something in their lives taught children how to cope without it, and then in the future, if things went tits up, they'd know how to cope with *that*, too. Like the old biddy in the attic. He'd coped with all of it. Even coped with prison.

Timmons came shuffling in, the soles of his slippers scraping on the carpet. The sound got on Mint's nerves, but he wouldn't show it. He was playing the long game here, or a shorter version if he could manage it, where Timmons carked it—but not before Mint had made sure the house was also being left to him.

You had to cover your own back when you didn't have anyone else to do it.

"Here you are, son."

The old man placed a tray on the coffee table with coffee in a brown cup with a monkey face on the side, the handle its tail, and a sandwich, white bread (which pissed him off), containing thick rashers of bacon. Now *that* he wasn't going to complain about. Brown sauce dripped out of one corner. Mint's mouth watered.

"Cheers." He sat up, taking care not to pull his stitches, grimacing anyway so he'd garner some sympathy.

"Do you need any more painkillers?" Timmons asked.

"Not long had some, ta."

Timmons sat in the armchair by the fireplace. "Them twins were here."

Mint was just about to take a bite out of his sandwich but paused. "What? Why didn't you say sooner?"

"What does it matter to you whether they were here or not? Or are you up to no good again?"

"A man's got to earn a living."

"You earn enough from the houses, you don't need to earn any more, and it's not like you pay tax on the rents you receive, is it. They're classed as earnings as well, you know, or I suppose you could claim you were unaware of that because you're a private landlord with no one advising you. Whatever, all I'm saying is that you've got more than enough. You could afford to live in a little house of your own instead of shacking up with your old man."

Mint hadn't told him he was 'shacking up' here because it was somewhere to hide, a place no one would think he'd be. He doubted anyone would *choose* to live with someone over seventy, with all those dribbles of piss landing on the toilet seat and not being cleaned up, then there were the drips on the floor. But Mint would put up with it and do the housework, and then when this gaff belonged to him he'd get new bog seats.

Sometimes you had to wade through the quagmire before you reached the paradise shore. He smiled to himself at that one. He should have been some kind of poet. Maybe he was in a former life.

"So what did the twins want?" Mint asked, nervous in case they'd found out he lived here.

"They were being good citizens and doing me a favour actually. Someone must have told them that I've been complaining to the new neighbours about the position of the bins. They wanted to know what it was all about, then they went next door and sorted it."

"How do you know they sorted it?"

"I nipped out the back and listened at the fence. Nosed through a hole, didn't I, and saw them sitting at one of them island wotsits."

Mint used to have a fancy island wotsit. Ashley had begged him for it, and he'd thrown two grand at her to get one, just to shut up her whiny voice. He'd only married her to make himself look respectable anyway, but he was paying for it. Three grand a month since his sentencing for the "shame" and "embarrassment" of her husband being a criminal. She really was a dickhead, all fancy hair and false nails, skyscraper high heels, and short dresses. Nothing but a tart, really, but she'd played the part of a trophy wife well. Of course she had, because he'd given her the high life.

"What was said?" Mint asked.

"I only caught a couple of bits before one of them shut the bloody back door. Something about swollen ankles."

"What?"

"The woman, she's pregnant. Didn't you notice when you went round to have a word? Her fella's Irish, a wiry little bastard who looks like he'd cut your head off rather than pass the time of day."

"I haven't spent enough time out in the street to have seen him. I do my job, get home, that's it."

"If you're doing the same job as you did before you went inside, then you'd do well to monitor your surroundings, especially where you live. You never know who you live by, son."

"I just thought you'd have told me if there was anyone dodgy I needed to be aware of."

"Those two next door are new, and it takes time to get to know someone. I've tested the type of people they are by bringing up the bins in conversation, then I was prepared to give them the benefit of the doubt for two more weeks, but if they kept leaving them in front of that bloody wall, I'd have contacted the twins myself."

"Have you considered the fact had nobody called them on your behalf?"

"What are you on about? They specifically came about the *bins*."

"So they said…"

"Are you trying to tell me something, boy?"

Mint had gone too far, thinking about himself rather than what Timmons would pick up on. He really didn't need him poking into his business. Already he'd twigged that Mint had gone back to selling drugs, and he'd known that's what he did before because he'd admitted to keeping an eye on him as he'd been growing up. That had given Mint the collywobbles, knowing someone had been observing him and he hadn't known it. How many other people had done the same to him? *Were* doing the same? It was a given the twins were watching him, that warning with the stabbing had been plain enough, but to actually come here, where he lived…

He ate his sandwich and drank his coffee while Timmons snored in his chair, then he got up and carried the tray into the kitchen. He stacked the plate and cup in the dishwasher, putting the tray down the side of the washing machine where the others belonged. At the back door, he thought about how Timmons had spied yesterday. He stepped outside, checking the upper windows of next door before he approached the fence. With no one watching him, as far as he was aware, he looked through a hole in the wood, having a direct line of sight to a back door and a window.

The woman sat at the island, thumbing through a magazine, a slanted diagonal shaft of July sun lighting up one of her shoulders, her face, and a very juicy boob. He hadn't had sex in ages, something Ashley had been good for, at least, but there was no way she'd let him anywhere near her now. There had been talk in prison that there was a sex parlour behind The Angel pub, a word-of-mouth establishment where you had to give your details and phone number if you wanted to use the services. He was tempted to go, using Timmons's info, obviously not showing a driver's licence or anything that had the old boy's age on it. One of Mint's cellmates from over the years had told him to drop his name at the reception, because then he'd definitely get in.

He'd do that after the little visit he needed to pay someone at lunchtime. It killed two birds with one stone because he'd be hungry again by then, so he could stop for something to eat.

He resumed watching the woman, who drank her coffee in such a way that he reckoned she had breeding. One of those posh types. That was probably why she'd ignored Timmons about the bins. Well-to-do people didn't follow the same rules as everybody else, did they.

Mint imagined making her do as she was told, his dick hardening. Maybe he'd keep an eye out on the neighbours after all, especially to see when the Irishman came and went. It would be interesting to note the times the woman was left at home alone.

Chapter Seven

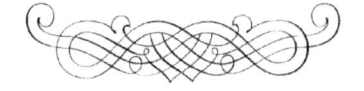

The kids were staying with their dad until next week. They enjoyed it there anyway and liked his girlfriend. Sharon had been jealous of that at first, but when she'd thought about it properly, wasn't it better that the kids had another mother figure, one who truly cared about them, especially if at any moment their real mother might not be around anymore? And she wasn't talking about walking away and abandoning them, it was death she worried about.

The thought of tears streaking their little faces because she was dead…

Maybe she shouldn't have had children when she'd known she might have a target on her back. All right, it wouldn't be there if she hadn't dobbed Mint in, but he wasn't to know it was her because she'd done it anonymously. But it was obvious, and he'd had plenty of time to stew on it while in the nick. To stew on how he could make her pay.

She stood at the café window with a cleaning cloth in one hand and a fake loaf in the other, absently wiping over the plastic crust while staring outside at the shoppers. She'd been doing that for the past couple of days, trying to catch sight of him before he caught sight of her, but she kept reminding herself that he might even have had to stay in hospital because of the stab wound. Or he could have died.

That would be nice.
Stop it.

She put the bread back and picked up a lemon, peering over at where he'd got stabbed. What had he been doing selling drugs on the street anyway? He must have had to start again after coming out of prison. Had someone taken care of his side business, renting out rooms to druggies? Had someone else taken over his drug patch? Or, God forbid, he'd moved to the Cardigan Estate—as in proper moved, relocated.

The not knowing bothered her so much that she wished she could get hold of him to talk about it, to see if he was after her. Although she'd been scared to in the past, she had confronted him on a couple of occasions.

She could do it again.

She still had his phone number but doubted it would be in use anymore, unless a family member or whatever had kept it going. That was the thing, she didn't know an awful lot about him, yet she'd bet he knew a damn sight more about her. He'd always had the upper hand—until the two times he hadn't. She'd been the one in the driver's seat then.

She put the lemon back in the basket, about to pick up another when she spotted him. She'd known she would if she hung around in the window for long enough every day. She thought through what she'd do to him, and the main scenario involved her running out amongst the shoppers, stabbing him, finishing the job the other bloke had started. But there'd be witnesses, and she'd end up going to prison herself.

Instead, she watched him. He stopped outside Home Bargains and stared across, startled at catching her staring. Was he frightened of her? Surely not. He seemed to give himself a mental talking-to, maybe debating whether to keep walking or to stop and gawp. She sucked in a breath at him walking across the street, weaving between shoppers, wincing a couple of times where his stab wound probably hurt. He reached her side of the street and stood on the pavement directly outside the café, staring straight into her eyes. He nodded, maybe to confirm to himself that he'd made the correct identification—yes, it was her—then raised his eyebrows. Was he asking her to come out? She shook her head. If he wanted to talk to her then it would be on her terms and her turf.

He approached the door.

Sharon took a few deep breaths to steady her nerves—she didn't want her voice to falter when they spoke to one another. He mustn't know—couldn't know—she was worrying about his intentions. If he spotted a weakness in her façade, he'd poke a finger in the crack and rip it until it became a big gaping hole.

He walked in, looking similar to the past in his clothing choice, his hair still slicked back, although grey streaked it now. He'd gained a few wrinkles on his face, particularly around the eyes, and she'd bet that wasn't from smiling. She doubted he'd had much to smile about where he'd been, unless he'd worked miracles and become a drug dealer inside, too. It wouldn't surprise her.

He sat in the corner, and she took one of the tablets off the counter by the till and went over there to take his order. It was weird standing by him again, except this time she looked down on him as he looked up. They studied each other for a moment, her cheeks burning with the humiliation his smirk had brought about—he had to be thinking that she'd let herself go.

"What can I get you?" she asked.

"I'll have a latte, a tuna sandwich with red onion and mayo, brown bread, and a slice of orange cake for afterwards, but I'd like it all delivered at the same time, please."

She automatically pressed the tablet screen to put his order in, then hit the SEND button. "Anything else?"

"A little chat wouldn't go amiss. And I'm not paying for that food and drink."

"I didn't think you would." She sat opposite him, glad that for once the closest two tables weren't occupied, only the third had a student type sitting there with his headphones on, watching something on YouTube. It wouldn't be long before they were joined by other customers, though, so he'd better make it quick or talk in code. "What's your issue, then?"

"Was it you?"

She frowned. "Was it me what?"

"You know what."

"I don't."

"The police, the second time. The tip-off."

She laughed quietly. "Why is it always me you blame, when like I told you before, I'm not going to want to involve myself with the police because of the ramifications it could have had for me if they started questioning me again. We've been through this. I don't even know what the second tip-off was about," she lied.

"The drugs. I went to prison. Don't make out you didn't know."

"How long did you go down for?"

"Seven years. And speaking of Seven, how is he?"

"I haven't spoken to him in years."

"Hmm. I've got no problem with him."

"But you have with me, even though I haven't done anything. That's nice for you, a complete waste of time to fill your mind with whatever it is you think about when you think of me, but I assure you, I had no hand in either of those phone calls to the police, and I haven't given the past the time of day ever since I moved away. As far as I was concerned, we'd come to an agreement, all three of us, that night when we met round the back of the chippy."

"I thought the same until the coppers knocked on my door to say they'd raided my garage."

"What, like a petrol station? I knew you rented out rooms in houses but I didn't know about the garage."

"No, it's a garage for a car except I didn't put the car in it." He leaned back and stared at her. "You really didn't know, did you."

Yes. "No."

He scrubbed a hand over his face. "The service in here is pretty shit. You put that order in a while ago."

"All the sandwiches are made from scratch."

"By the looks of things, she's making the fucking cake from scratch an' all." He sat up straighter. "Ah, here she comes."

Melanie placed a tray on the table, apologising for the time it had taken to make the sandwich. "We had no red onion left, so I had to nip over to Home Bargains and buy one for you."

"That's service and a half, that is," Mint said. "I take back what I just said to your colleague here."

Melanie smiled. "Is there anything else I can get for you, sir?"

"No thanks."

She walked away. Mint picked up his sandwich, inspected the contents, nodded, then bit into it. It was bread from the bakery which they cut themselves, so he had a proper doorstep going on. He was probably going to make her wait for the entire time it took for him to eat the food, but that was okay, she could sit here and take a load off while he thought he was either preventing her from getting on or she'd get in trouble for slacking off. She had no intention of letting him know she was the manager unless she had to.

It took ten minutes before he licked the last of the orange-flavoured icing off his finger and thumb tips and another couple for him to drink half the coffee. During that time she'd ordered herself a cappuccino and had drunk it.

"So, you're out," she said, just for something to say.

"Obviously. Part of it was for good behaviour, the other part was getting turfed out so bigger criminals could be let in. In other words, overcrowding."

"Is there a special someone?"

"No. I don't trust women anymore."

"Did you go back to the same area?"

"No. The estate agent I worked for didn't want me back, and as for the drugs, I didn't want to risk peddling where I'd been nicked, so I came over here. Someone else runs the houses for me."

"Did you get permission from the twins to peddle?"

"No." His expression clouded over. "As a matter of fact, that's why I got stabbed. A little warning, I imagine, that if I don't start paying up or stop selling drugs on their precious Estate then worse will come my way."

"And you're prepared to do that. To keep selling."

"What can I say, I like the high life."

"And the rents you get aren't enough?"

"There are different degrees of high life, and the one I get with just the rents isn't the one I want. Anyway, why are you asking? Are you thinking of ringing the police on me again?"

She sighed as though he bored her. "This is the last time I'm going to say it, but I didn't phone the police and I won't be phoning them in the future. I couldn't care less *what* you were doing."

"Do you need any gear?"

"I stopped that years ago around the time we moved out of your house."

"So what about you? Got a bloke? Any kids?"

"What do you care?"

He shrugged. "Just making polite conversation."

"Are you checking whether I've got a fella who can protect me from you?"

He smiled and stood. "It's always handy to be informed of that sort of thing. Thanks for the lunch."

He walked out, going across the street to the left and disappearing down the alley beside Superdrug. She sat there and contemplated the conversation for a moment, peeking between the lines and replaying what they'd talked about to see whether there had been any implied threats anywhere. The only one she could find was what he'd said just before he'd gone, as if he'd wanted to know if she had some form of protection because he planned on doing something to her.

She stood and cleared the table, taking the tray to hand it off to a member of staff. She popped the tablet in her apron pocket and returned to the table to give it a wash, turning afterwards to check the street through the window. He wasn't out there.

She had a couple of options: let the twins know that he had no intention of paying them protection money and would continue to sell drugs on Cardigan, or she could do what she'd wanted to in the past and kill him. There was no

Seven in her ear to talk her out of it this time, but her conscience piped up in his place: *You've got kids now. Don't be so stupid.*

And if she wanted him dead, it was better to go to the twins. It would mean explaining everything, though, and because none of what had happened years ago had been on Cardigan, she doubted very much they'd give a shit anyway. But she was a resident now, and maybe what affected her was important to them, no matter where it had gone on.

But was she prepared to reopen old wounds and admit to what a cow she'd been? They had a certain view of her, and she didn't want that to get tainted.

So that means Mint stays alive.

She *tsked* at herself. She'd give it some more thought before she made a decision. Rome wasn't built in a day.

Chapter Eight

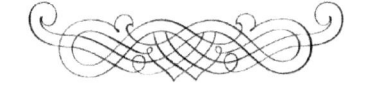

Charlotte didn't see Grace again until two days after they'd been to her house. It was Saturday morning, and Mint had messaged her to go and sit in the attic room until eleven, then she had to make herself scarce. She didn't want to have to tell Grace that Pip was dead, but she'd forced herself to. Grace had cried, saying she'd had a feeling her bird wouldn't have been

cared for, considering there was no one to care for him. She'd slept for an hour afterwards and had only just woken up again, her top eyelids puffy and red in her pale-as-parchment face. Her skin looked so thin, as though it would rip if she caught one of her long nails on it.

Charlotte hadn't questioned who was taking Grace to the toilet, who was washing her, changing her clothes and the bedding, because she'd assumed it was the fake nephew, but Mint had said he only visited in the mornings and late evenings, so how was she going to the loo during the day? Was Mint coming here?

The least she knew the better, although that was easier said than done. She found herself wanting *to know the answers, to unravel the mystery, but then wasn't it best that the police did it? If she could get that jewellery appraised and sold, the evidence of being in Grace's house would no longer be here, so the police coming wouldn't be a problem.*

But would *they have to come here? Not if Charlotte could get Grace out and ask the police to meet them in a safe place. But what could she say in order to make them understand the urgency, that someone responsible needed to take care of Grace instead of her being kept in the attic? There was no way Charlotte could admit to knowing that the old woman was going to be murdered. She'd be classed as an accessory. Maybe she could say she'd gone to Grace's house, like she'd been asked, and everything was dusty, the bird was dead, and for some reason Mint had turned up.*

How would she account for not calling the police sooner?

She swore under her breath.

"What's the matter?" Grace asked.

"How come you're even here?" *That was the only way Charlotte could think to put it so it would look like she didn't know. She wasn't about to sit there and tell Grace,* "Oh, you're here because you're going to get murdered…" *But what she was trying to get out of the old woman was how she'd come to be here. Who'd brought her?*

"It's a hospice," Grace said, "and I'm not very well."

"What's wrong with you?"

"I'm not sure. I'm never awake for long enough to ask or to even see a nurse. Can you do it for me, ask?"

Charlotte nodded because she didn't want to verbalise a promise she couldn't keep. There were no nurses, this was all a setup, and it was starting to feel bloody horrible now that she'd seen Grace as a human being.

"Who brought you here?" Charlotte asked. *"Was it your nephew?"*

Grace frowned. "I told you, I don't have a nephew. I can't remember how I got here. I woke up here, and then you came in and told me you were going to sit with me for a bit. I felt so tired. I always feel so tired…"

That would be the drugs then.

"What's the last thing you remember before you came here?"

Grace stared at the ceiling for a long time. "Someone was coming round for dinner. It was the person who wanted to sell the house for me. I was going to downsize, it's always been too big, and since I was there on my own, I thought it best to get rid."

"Who was it?"

"An estate agent."

"So did you contact him first, or did he contact you?"

"I didn't contact him at all. We met in the little shop around the corner. I was talking to John behind the counter about selling up, and this man butted in and said he was an estate agent. We went outside for a chat, sat on the bench there, and he handed me a card with his phone number on it."

"Did it also say his name and that he was an estate agent?"

"No. He said he was freelance and that the phone number was also his personal one, so he didn't want to have his name or whatever on the card. I shrugged it off; young people are so strange these days."

Young? "How old was he then?"

"Forty? Something like that."

Charlotte supposed forty would seem young to someone in their eighties. "What did he look like?"

"He had a nice suit on, black hair all swept back. His name's Reggie Smith. He reminded me of my husband when we were younger."

Charlotte thought back to the photograph in the summer house. The husband loosely looked like Mint. That fucking bastard had tricked her. He was the one coming morning and night to see to her in the attic.

Reggie Smith, my arse.

"When I went to the house to feed Pip…" Charlotte took a deep breath. "There were place settings for two people at your dining table. Is that something you do in general, leaving it out on display, or…"

"I don't recall eating, but no, I don't generally leave it out. Think of the dust!"

"What did you cook?"

"I didn't. I ordered Italian food to be delivered. It came about ten minutes before he did, and I remember popping it in the oven on low for it to keep warm."

"So you remember him arriving?"

"Oh yes. He bought some wine with him, plus champagne glasses, and we toasted to him being able to get a good price for the house. I drank the whole glass, and I don't remember anything after that until I woke up here."

So the clever fucker had brought his own glasses, there would be no trace of her drinking bubbly that had been tampered with, and she'd probably passed out, making it easy for him to scoop her up and take her away. Had he waited until it was dark and then carried her out the front, or had he parked round the back in the street behind and gone that way?

There was no doubt in Charlotte's mind that it was Mint, and if he'd used his own vehicle to transport Grace then it was going to be easy for the police to find out that he'd abducted her from her home, but if he'd had a car stolen, which, let's face it, wasn't beyond the realms of possibility, considering who he sold drugs to, then there wouldn't be any proof that he'd done anything wrong. Unless his mug had been caught on camera. He hadn't hidden who he was when he'd approached the house the other night, so it was obvious he didn't care that he'd be spotted.

Maybe he really was an estate agent.

Charlotte was about to chat to Grace about that, but the old woman had fallen asleep again. With ten minutes left before she had to leave, she listened to the tick of the clock and wondered whether it was an irritation or a comfort to Grace in the darkness when she woke.

Eleven o'clock arrived, and Charlotte adjusted the quilt over Grace so it fitted snugly. She resisted peeking underneath to see if a catheter had been placed. Surely it had, but didn't that mean Mint would need help from an actual nurse or someone in the know in order for it to be fitted? Grace never complained about having wet sheets or nightclothes, so she was definitely doing her business somehow.

Charlotte left the room before she drove herself mad with the questions she had no answers to. And did she really want answers? No, she just wanted to get that jewellery sold.

She went downstairs, tiptoeing past Seven's door; she didn't want him to ask where she was going. She took the next flight down to her floor, went to the cubbyhole in the chimney to take out the jewellery she'd placed in a little velvet bag, then popped it in her pocket and left the house.

She walked to the bus stop, running the last bit—a bus had drawn up. She rushed to get on, sitting at the back and staring out of the window to prevent anybody trying to strike up a conversation. She'd found the older generation tended to do that, and it would remind her of sitting with Grace, and then the guilt would come because she had the woman's possessions in her pocket. Stolen possessions.

She got off at the depot, moving along to one of the other bus stops that would take her ten miles away to a pawnbroker she'd looked up on Google using the computer at work. She'd cleared the cookies afterwards, thinking it best in case she did phone the police about Grace and they decided to poke into Charlotte's life. The next bus was due in fifteen minutes, so she quickly nipped into the newsagent's shop to buy herself a meal deal for lunch. She was tempted to get some cigarettes, but wasn't that just switching one bad habit for another? Or was it better to smoke so she focused on that rather than the lack of cocaine?

Fuck it, she bought twenty Benson and Hedges, almost fainting at the price. At that cost she was going to have to smoke every now and again when things got really bad rather than have a twenty-a-day habit like she used to. Once outside, she shoved the cigarettes in her other pocket, abandoning the idea of smoking any at all but telling herself that as long as she had some, then she'd feel safer somehow.

The bus had arrived early, so she boarded and moved halfway along, sitting close to the window and putting her carrier bag from the shop on the seat beside her. She took a sandwich out and ate that, and by the time she was finished, the journey had begun.

It went quicker than she'd thought. She got off, patting her pocket to make sure the jewellery was still in there, then putting the carrier bag of empty packaging in a nearby bin. She'd had a Fanta with the meal deal so needed the toilet. She found one in the bus station, surprised how clean it was compared to the depot at home. Maybe she ought to move here instead of remaining in the area where she currently lived. Using Google Maps, she walked towards town thinking that the East End wasn't so bad at all.

She found the pawnbroker's tucked down a stone-paved alley. Instead of the bay window she'd imagined, the front was a flat pane spanning the whole width apart from where the door was. She stepped inside, nervous but telling herself she had to pretend she wasn't. If she wanted to sell this gear then she was going to have to make out she had the right to sell it.

No other customers were around. A blonde woman stood behind the counter, about fifty, prim and proper *in her suit jacket, giving the impression she was too snooty to accept anything that might have come her way by foul means. Charlotte's stomach turned over, and she almost bottled it.*

"Can I help?" the woman asked, her accent as rough as a badger's arse, completely at odds with how she looked. "Buying or selling?"

"Selling."

"Let's have a butcher's then."

Charlotte walked up to the counter and pulled her hand out of her pocket, placing the velvet bag on the glass counter.

"Before I open the bag, where have these come from? And I want the honest truth. If they're nicked I'll probably still buy them, but I like to know if they're nicked so I know I need to take the gems out of the settings."

Charlotte blinked in surprise. How did she know she wasn't a police officer? Maybe it was Charlotte's skittish demeanour that gave away the fact she was crapping her pants.

"I got it from an old woman," Charlotte said. It wasn't a lie.

"With or without her permission?"

"She…um…she isn't aware that I have them yet."

"Nice way of putting it. Very diplomatic." The woman pulled gloves on, placed a mouse pad down, and opened the bag, tipping the contents out. She stared at the haul for a few moments. *"Give me a minute or so to have a proper look, will you?"*

Charlotte waited, assuming that the binocular thingy the woman used was to check if the diamonds and whatever were real.

"I'd love to tell you these are worth a fortune, but I'm afraid the best offer I can give you is five grand."

That was more than Charlotte had been expecting, and she choked back a response of, "Fuck me!" Instead, she said, "Thank you, that's lovely," Not even caring if she was being swindled.

"I shall remove the stones from the settings, just to be on the safe side." She put the jewellery back in the bag, turned, and unlocked a safe behind a painting on the wall, which she'd opened like a door. She put the bag in and took a stack of notes out, locking the safe. She counted five thousand pounds out, stuck an elastic band around it, and handed it to Charlotte. *"Nice doing business with you."*

Charlotte smiled her thanks and left, rushing to the bus stop, thankful she only had ten minutes to wait.

The journey home was full of her working out what she'd do with that money plus what she had in the chimney. There was enough for a deposit and three months' rent in advance now, so when she got back she was going to go, ironically, to an estate agent to see if there were any homes available to rent. She asked herself if she was going to tell Seven that she was moving earlier than they'd planned—he'd perhaps ask how they could afford to go yet. She could tell him that her parents had lent her the money, but maybe that would look a bit too obvious on the back of being at Grace's house.

Would he suspect she'd stolen something?

Chapter Nine

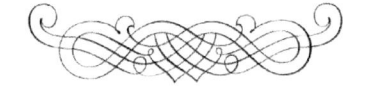

That little meeting had gone well. Charlotte was always such a brash cow, and if she didn't look such a dog these days, Mint would consider hooking up with her until he found something better on offer, but then she wasn't exactly the type to take him up on it. She'd probably rather die than fuck him. What a state she'd become. A fucking shame, that, because she'd been such a tasty bird once upon a time. He reckoned she must have sampled a bit too many slices of the cake she served to customers for her body to have gone to the dogs like that.

And what a comedown that must be, working in café when she was in a solicitor's office before. Or was that an accountant's? He couldn't remember, exactly, but his point was that she'd once been pretty high up on the 'winning at life' scale, and now look at her.

He believed her though—again—that she hadn't gone to the police about him. She was always so convincing when he confronted her, so nothing had changed there. It was easier to blame her because that would make sense, but when he was faced with trying to work out who it was *other* than her, it threw him for a loop. Seven wouldn't have done it, he was a bloody wimp, always letting her do the talking for him, but it could have been Polly, wreaking havoc behind bars of her own.

That fucking Polly. He should never have got involved with her.

He walked in the direction Google Maps had shown him on his phone. There were a few streets that had nice pads on this housing estate, but others were rough, like the ones in the road he'd grown up in. That reminded him, he still had to visit his mother, but his dick came first, and it kept stiffening for attention. He thought about saggy, wrinkly tits to stop himself becoming aroused, finally approaching the street he needed.

Several women stood on the corner, some tarted up, others in more understated clothing, but it was obvious what they were all there for. One of them spoke to a man; she leaned into his car window, one leg cocked, arse out, classic prostitute pose. He didn't want to have to go down that route, these women were probably dirty as eff down below, so he continued on towards The Angel.

A man stood in an alleyway on the other side of the road, staring Mint's way. What was wrong with him, was he too embarrassed to approach the slags? Or was he building up the courage to go into the pub and talk to the receptionist at the parlour? Mint wasn't even sure whether he was supposed to just go down that corridor with a camera at the end or ask someone at the bar first, his cellmate hadn't given specific instructions.

Mint pushed the door open and walked in, doing what Timmons had advised, scoping out his surroundings. To the left, lots of round tables for two or three people and some slot machines. Ahead, a long bar. To the right, more tables, a big clock with numbers large enough for even drunk people to make out, and in the top-right corner, double doors, a sign with Toilets above it. He remembered that part of the instructions so headed that way, finding himself in a wide corridor, doors leading to the toilets and another marked Private. He tried that door, even though he reckoned it would be locked, but it opened. He quickly dipped into the corridor his cellmate had described—apparently, not all customers were aware it existed, and he'd said the rule was to be fast when entering so no one saw him.

An automatic light went on, and he walked down the corridor towards another door, the camera positioned above the lintel to the right. He pressed the doorbell on the frame.

"Yes?" a woman asked, her voice disembodied.

"I've been sent here by Buzzy Gizzard."

"Hang on."

Maybe she was checking the list of customers to see if Buzzy even existed. He'd better, Mint would be well naffed off for being sent on a wild goose chase as a joke. And it wasn't like he could get the bloke back for it either, because he wasn't due out of prison for another ten years, and Mint was fucked if he'd bother going there to visit him. Too much hassle.

"What's your name, address, and phone number?" the woman asked.

"Peter Timmons, twelve Duke's Way." He rattled off his own mobile number.

"Two seconds."

This was the bit where he felt under scrutiny. What if they had some sort of special database where they could access details of people on it and they'd know he wasn't Timmons because he was nowhere near seventy years old?

"Your membership is pending while we do some further checks," she said. "You'll get a text message if you're welcome to come back."

If I'm welcome to come back? Fucking cheek. I'd be paying good money to use one of their slappers. What kind of place is this where they turn customers away?

He hated not being allowed to be a part of something exclusive. It made him feel less than, left out, bullied in a way, the boy who wasn't permitted to join in the fun.

"Cheers," he said, sounding affable but feeling anything but. He smiled, gave the camera wave, and walked back through the pub. There was no way they'd get his custom now, maybe not even if he was accepted into the parlour, so he'd go for a pint elsewhere. Maybe he'd get lucky and pick some woman up for free.

He stepped outside and glanced down the street. Thought about dipping his wick in one of those tarts on the corner, but his thought from earlier about them being dirty put him off. He went the other way, following Google Maps again as he wasn't familiar with this part of Cardigan. He ended up back in town inside the Red Lion, fully aware he was close to Charlotte in the Shiny Fork but unable to see her. That was all right, he'd see her later when she left the café. In the meantime, he'd drink a pint of lager and think about whether having sex with her would *really* be so bad. If he closed his eyes, he could pretend she looked the same as she used to.

He waited at the end of town by the taxi rank, standing partially behind a Transit that had parked beside a hole in the ground with a workmen's cordon around it. Looked like a possible water pipe leak. He checked his watch; he'd noted the opening and closing times for the Shiny Fork, so he reckoned she'd be another minute or so. From where he stood he couldn't see the high street without leaving the safety of his hiding place, only the back road behind the café side was visible, but it was okay, she was coming along there now, heading straight for him. He remembered she used to drive back in the day, but maybe she was down on her luck these days and couldn't afford a car. But she could afford a taxi, because she beelined for the one at the head of the queue.

He stepped out from behind the van, waving and smiling. "Blimey, fancy seeing you here."

She glared at him; she knew damn well he'd known she'd be there. "Stalker much?"

"Don't be like that, I just happened to be here, I swear."

"Why don't I believe you? Um, maybe because we've been down this road before. I really don't understand why you can't get it into your head that I'm not interested in what you did back then, or what you're doing now. We've both moved on, we've got lives to lead, and honest to God, if you keep appearing, I'm going to tell my bosses."

"Those twins?"

"Yes."

"Look, I promise you I just want to talk. I haven't made friends with anyone since I moved to Cardigan. You're the only friendly face I know. Or friendly-ish anyway. That scowl of yours might beg to differ."

She shook her head, obviously exasperated with him. "What do you want?"

"Just a drink, maybe some dinner. A chat. Something. Anything."

"Are you seriously saying that you'd rather sit in a pub with me than go home?"

"I don't really have a home anymore. The wife's got it."

"I didn't know you were married."

"I never felt the need to broadcast it. So what do you reckon, should we go to the Red Lion? I've just been in there for a pint, and it's an all-right place."

She sighed and looked to the bright-blue sky, her lips clamped together, then she focused on him. "You're lucky I've got nothing to do this evening and can't be arsed to cook."

He was more inclined to think she didn't want to get in the taxi, giving him the opportunity to get in the one behind and follow her, finding out where she lived. But she was unaware that he knew where she lived already, having followed her yesterday. "Fair enough. Come on."

He crossed the street, glancing over his shoulder to see if she was actually coming. She was the type to jump in the taxi while his back was turned and fuck off quick. But she was there, hefting a bag strap onto her shoulder, trotting to keep up. He wasn't sure he was going to be able to go through with seducing her—she wasn't slim enough for him, was no longer his type at all. What a waste of a good body. She'd gone and ruined it.

They walked down the high street, past a pizza restaurant and a kebab shop. She hung slightly behind him, as if embarrassed to be by his side, taking her phone out of her bag and clutching it to her chest. She didn't trust him, that much was obvious, but it might change after two or three gins. He was determined to get her to think he was a nice bloke underneath it all, have a few more drinking sessions with her to really cement their friendship, then she might let her guard down.

He wanted to know all she would tell him about the twins.

They sat and chatted for a good while, stilted conversation that made him uncomfortable because it was obvious she was only sitting there on sufferance. After two small glasses of wine mixed with lemonade, she declined to have any more, so that put paid to his idea of getting her drunk. She seemed to want to keep her wits about her at all times, but maybe that was only because she was in his company.

"I'm going to get off," she said once they'd finished their pie and chips.

"I'll walk you home."

"No thanks, I prefer to keep my address private."

"What do you think I'm going to do?"

She stood and stared down at him. "Think about it…it shouldn't be too hard to wonder why I don't want you anywhere near my place."

He knew exactly what she was talking about and almost laughed but held it back. "I was a different person when I did that."

"Prison reform you, did it?"

He leaned back, making out she'd defeated him. "Don't blame me if something happens to you on your way home, then."

"Is that a threat?"

"God, no! Where do you get all these ideas from that I'm out to hurt you?"

"I wonder…"

She strutted away, her stride confident, and left the pub. He really did want to go after her, to get a shag no matter that her body didn't do it for him, but he had to think about her working for the twins (or was she lying about that?).

He had another pint and then walked home, catching sight of the pregnant woman who lived next door. She stood in a top window, raising one hand to draw the curtains, even though with it being summer it was still light out. He imagined her getting into bed, her belly swollen from the baby, and his desire for her petered out.

He was going to have to use his hand again.

He let himself in, cringing at the sound of Timmons shuffling from his chair to come and greet him in the hallway, something he had a habit of doing as though Mint was eight years old and needed chivvying into a bath and then bed.

"Nice evening?" Timmons asked.

"Yeah, had a couple of pints with an old friend."

"Who?"

"You wouldn't know her."

"Oh, a her, is it?" Timmons waggled his straggly grey eyebrows. "Did you walk her home?"

"I offered, but she didn't want me to."

"Better luck next time, son." Timmons laughed.

Mint wanted to punch him.

"I had another visit from the twins while you were out." The old man slip-slid his way into the kitchen, taking the kettle off its base and filling it at the sink.

Mint stared after him from his spot in the hallway. "What did they want this time?"

"They were making enquiries about me, although I quickly got the gist that they meant you. Do you want to tell me what you've been up to, or shall I remind you?"

"What are you on about?" Mint stomped into the kitchen, leaning against the worktop in front of the under-counter fridge, his arms folded in defence.

"They showed me a picture. Of you."

"Eh?"

"Standing in front of their camera in a corridor at the back of The Angel. Has that jogged your memory?"

"Oh…"

"Hmm, they were letting me know that someone was using my identity to try and secure a *fuck*."

Taken aback by the ferocity spat out in that one word, Mint stared at Timmons. "They have my phone number, so there was no need for them to come round here."

"But the thing is, something you don't know about the twins is that they seem to find things out no matter how hard you try to hide them. They don't own the parlour or the pub, but they're heavily involved in making sure everything runs smoothly there. Now I wasn't aware of this until they told me, but they have an app on their phones that shows them who looks up into that camera. Now, the woman who did the initial check on the information you gave her discovered that your face didn't match my age, so of course, she knew someone was trying to get in under false pretences, so she let the twins know what time you visited. They checked the stored footage on the app, saw your mug, twinned it with this address, and now think you're a miscreant who just so happened to use my address—at least I hope they do and they don't cotton on to the fact that I lied to them. I said I lived alone, because *you* said you didn't want anyone to know where you were. Imagine my surprise—or maybe I shouldn't have been surprised—when they said they were the ones who'd organised for you to be stabbed because you were misbehaving on their manor."

Timmons ignored the fact the kettle had clicked off. He shuffled closer to Mint.

"What did I tell you when you moved in? No trouble on my doorstep. Yet here we are. If those Brothers come round here one more time regarding you, you're going to have to leave. You earn enough money, you know how estate agents work, so get looking for somewhere else, because soon the neighbours are going to be asking me questions about why we've had leaders in our street, specifically at my door, and I've always prided myself on being a decent person, and you…you're making me look bad."

"Give me a month and I'll be gone. They have checks for everything these days, much more than before, and I keep getting turned down every time I apply for flats."

"That's because you've been in the nick. I know they say they're not supposed to discriminate, but they do. Who the fuck wants a crim living in their house? And anyway, you've got rooms you can use in your own houses. Give a tenant two months' notice and turf them out."

"I've got attic space I can turn into a flat, it's actually being done at the moment, but it's not going to work, me living back on that Estate."

"Because you've got a target on your back. Well, you've gone and got yourself one here, too, so aren't you clever."

Timmons made tea, but only one cup, then he left the room. Mint pushed off the worktop and made himself a coffee, going to sit at the table instead of joining the old man in the living room. He probably wouldn't be welcome anyway.

He thought about the mess his life was in, and all because someone had phoned the police on him. When he found out who that was, they were going to be dead.

Providing his previous supplier didn't kill him first.

Chapter Ten

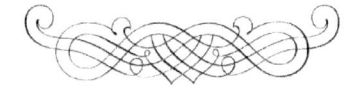

Moody sat outside Mr Timmons' house on surveillance. His missus had gone to bingo this evening, and she was staying overnight at her mum's south of the river, so it wasn't a hardship to sit here watching. He'd spotted Mint when he'd gone into the house, and before that he'd seen the twins arrive to speak to the old man.

They'd messaged him beforehand to let him know to ignore them. Apparently, this Mint fella had tried to get on the membership list for the parlour using his dad's name.

Moody had read quite the dossier on Mint. He'd been imprisoned for drug dealing in large amounts on the Greaves Estate, a small patch whose leader was old and let his son, Nathaniel, do all the hard graft. Mint had basically been doing whatever the hell he liked there, no one taking him to task, but then he'd been grassed up for the drugs and put away.

The twins had assumed he'd moved to Cardigan because he couldn't exactly live safely on Greaves—not with drug suppliers apparently still after him for the cocaine that had been seized by the police. Moody was surprised the outfit hadn't put the squeeze on him to sell his three Victorian houses in order to pay them back, but then if they couldn't find Mint, they couldn't squeeze him, could they.

If he hadn't become a blip on the twins' radar, no one on Cardigan would be any the wiser as to who he was, other than someone in a suit selling baggies. No one around here gave a shit about him except his father. His mother, Bridie, hadn't seen him since before he'd gone to prison, and as for his wife, Ashley, she didn't want anything more to do with him—and neither did his kids, sons who now called her new boyfriend Dad. They'd only been small when he'd been sentenced so probably didn't even remember him, poor little sods.

Some bloke managed Mint's tenants, and according to the people who rented the rooms, he was a good man and got repairs done the same day or the day after. He'd also got one of the residents pregnant, paid a large sum to keep her mouth shut, and stayed living with his wife as though nothing had happened, but it seemed as long as he was on the ball with leaky taps and broken boilers, no one paid his morals any mind.

All this information had come to light courtesy of Nathaniel who'd done his part in helping the twins, sending people around to ask the relevant questions. All in all, it was a mixed bag of info, all of it pointing to Mint being an utter twat who nobody particularly liked.

George had sent a message to say Mr Timmons wasn't his cup of tea, a bit smarmy and creepy, on the ball as to the goings-on in the street, a fair warning to Moody who might get seen, even though he sat behind the illegal-level blacked-out windows of a pretty impressive Jaguar E-PACE that was off to Spain come next week, sold to an ex-pat who didn't give a fuck where it had come from so long as it now belonged to him.

At just gone half ten, the front door opened. With the sunlight all but faded from the earlier, pink-tinted sky, a dark-grey hue in its place, plus the light on in the hallway, it was easy to see Mint standing there. He stepped out, shoving his hands in the hoodie pockets of his black tracksuit, closing the door and jogging down the short driveway and onto the pavement. He didn't get into any of the cars parked at the kerb.

Fuck it, Moody was going to have to get out and follow him.

MOODY: PURSUING SUBJECT ON FOOT. NEW MAN NEEDED TO WATCH HOUSE?

GG: NAH.

He waited for Mint to turn left at the corner, then he got out of the car. He kept well back, catching up to Mint and keeping him in his sights. Mint nipped across a small park, kicking what sounded like a can out of his path in the darkness, coming out into a residential street full of blocks of flats. He disappeared between two of them, and by the time Moody had managed to cross the road after a car had held him up, he couldn't see him anywhere. He stared across at a row of terraced homes. Maybe the bloke had gone into one of those, but Moody didn't think doing door-to-door enquiries without the twins' permission would be a good idea. In case he was being watched, he backed into the shadows and stood shielded by a large tree trunk, sending a message.

MOODY: TARGET FOLLOWED TO THE RIVER WALK HOUSING ESTATE. LOST HIM AS HE WENT BETWEEN BLOCKS OF FLATS IN FISH ROAD. NOW ON ANCHOR AVENUE, BUT NO SIGN OF HIM. HE COULD HAVE GONE INTO ANY OF THE HOUSES.

GG: WE'RE OUT AND ABOUT IN THE VAN. ON OUR WAY. STAY PUT.

Moody took a few steps back to lean against one of the flats beside a window covered with a lace curtain. Darkness lay beyond it, so he was safe from being spotted by the resident. It was shadowed here, the tree branches and thick leaves creating a dark patch, and in his black clothing he was relatively anonymous and indistinguishable. He kept darting his attention up and down the street, hoping to catch sight of Mint, but there was no movement apart from a woman coming out of one of the houses carrying a wailing toddler. She strapped it in a car seat and drove off, probably her last-ditch attempt to get the kid asleep before she lost her parental marbles.

Headlights entered the street from the left, and as the vehicle drew closer, Moody recognised the shape as that of the twins' van. It drew to a stop, and he pushed off the building, running across the grass and getting in the back. He shut the door and sat on the wheel arch. Ralph came over and flopped onto his feet for a fuss.

"Anything?" George asked.

"Just a woman taking her crying kid out."

"Maybe it copped a look at your face and bawled its eyes out."

Moody laughed, although it soon dried up to be replaced by sobriety. "I'm fucking pissed off I lost him."

"He's probably nipped out to sell some drugs," Greg said.

"Despite being stabbed as a warning not to do so," George said. "What a plonker. But if he is selling, then he'll come out of one of these houses any minute, unless he knew he was being followed and legged it up the street and into the next one before you got the chance to see where he'd gone."

"Which then means he knows damn well he shouldn't be doing what he's doing—the warning got through to him in that respect but didn't stop him from peddling, which was the whole point in knifing him in the first place."

George sighed. "You go back to the house, and we'll get someone to come and sit here for a bit. We'll drive around and see if we can spot him."

Moody got out of the van and made his way back to the Jaguar, hoping Mr Timmons didn't spot his return. He didn't fancy being hauled over the coals by an old man, not tonight.

Chapter Eleven

It had all happened so quickly. Charlotte had secured a two-bedroom flat, well affordable between her and Seven, although there was no way she could afford it on her own, so if he ever backed out she was going to have to get someone else in to take his place quickly. He'd swallowed her story about borrowing money from her parents, and they'd moved in two days after she'd walked into the estate agent's. Once she'd announced that she had five grand to pop down straight off the bat, the man had all but bitten off her hand, showing her what was on offer in the price range she and Seven had discussed.

Mint had been contacted for a reference, which could have been awkward, but they had both let him know they no longer needed rooms in the house, and apart from him muttering about needing someone to sit with Grace now that Charlotte wouldn't be around, he'd taken it really well. It made sense, she supposed, that he'd have a list of people as long as his arm to fill their empty rooms. They'd both already paid him rent till the end of the month, which was all he'd asked for instead of the two months' notice in the contract, which was weird, but he'd seemed super distracted and clearly wanted the conversation to come to an end.

"Jesus, I only dropped by to sell some drugs, not have a full-blown conversation with you two."

"Would you have preferred us to just bugger off in a moonlight flit?" Charlotte had blurted. "We could have done that, you know."

"Yeah, let's pretend I'm grateful. And what we talked about…" He'd stared hard at Charlotte, then at Seven. "About the old dear and what's going to happen to her."

Charlotte had become uneasy. "Yes…"

"It's between us and stays that way."

That had been the end of that conversation. He'd fucked off upstairs, presumably to deliver drugs, although he could well have gone to see Grace. Charlotte didn't know, she was too busy going back into her room to pack up her things. Thankfully, they'd been able to hire a van which fitted all of their stuff from their rooms in one go, and they'd dropped it all off at the flat, leaving it in a higgledy-piggledy mess so they could return to Mint's house and clean their old rooms.

Walking back in gave her a serious case of wanting to run and never come back. Especially because someone else was already lying on a single bed, some scrote with greasy brown hair and spots all over his cheeks.

"Who the fuck are you?" He propped himself up on one elbow. His eyebrows met in the middle where he frowned so hard.

"I should be asking you that, because this is technically still my room until the end of the month."

That fucking cheeky Mint had rented her space out already, yet they'd only told him a few hours ago they were leaving. Like she'd thought, he had no trouble keeping the rent pouring in.

The man sat up. He drew a big holdall towards him, as though protective of it, like she'd want to nick it. Or maybe he had stuff in there that was precious to him. "I'm renting it now. What do you want?"

"To clean it. That's part of the tenancy agreement before you leave."

"I thought it was clean enough myself, but be my guest."

How odd to scrub the room and en suite while he lounged around watching, but she got it done, handed him her keys, and walked out, going upstairs to see if Seven was ready or if he wanted some help. The sooner they got out of there, the sooner they could get things sorted in the new place, then she could phone the police anonymously and tell them about Grace.

She tapped on Seven's door, which was ajar, and her knocking pushed it open a bit more. He stood at the window staring out at the back garden, darting his head in her direction quickly as though he hadn't heard anyone coming in but had caught her movement in the corner of is eye. He lifted his finger to his lips and gestured for her to shut the door. She wanted to ask him what was going on, but the tilt of his head told her he was listening. Now Charlotte came to think of it, she could hear talking coming through the ceiling.

Who was upstairs with Grace? It sounded deep, like a man. Mint?

Seven suddenly paled. "We need to leave."

Charlotte glanced around at the tumbleweeds of dust on the floor and the general moving-out debris that had congregated at the edges of the skirting board and in the corners. "But you haven't even cleaned. Do you really want Mint coming after you? You know what he's like."

"He doesn't know where we've moved to."

"You can bet he'll find out—the estate agent asked him for a reference, remember. He could go there and force someone to tell him our address. Anyway, what's the matter? What did you hear?"

"I'm sure someone said this was the last night the old girl would be here."

"Shit."

"Look, let's just get this cleaned and then we can go. Whatever happens after that is none of our business."

Typical Seven, washing his hands of it. She wasn't even sure why she was friends with someone who didn't have a conscience, but then hers had conveniently slipped by the wayside when it suited her, so she was a fine one to talk.

Seven swept up while she cleaned his bathroom. Thank God they didn't have kitchens to deal with. They each shared one on the separate floors, and someone came in once a week to keep them clean and tidy. An hour later they were done, and they left Seven's room, Charlotte tempted to go upstairs to see Grace, but someone was coming down from up there. Seven hadn't shut his door yet, so she motioned for him to get back inside quickly. She closed the door until there was a little gap—she wanted to see who the hell had visited Grace.

Charlotte held back a gasp. It was a woman of around twenty-eight in a light-blue nurse's uniform, her ginger hair in a low bun, and a clipboard held to her chest with one arm. She breezed down the next set of steps. Charlotte waited for a while, then she left the room, going downstairs. She spotted the woman in the other stairwell, heading for the ground floor. Charlotte glanced back at Seven to make sure he was keeping up.

By the time they got down to the hallway, she looked out of the window beside the front door to find the woman was getting into a black car. Determined to find out what the hell was going on, Charlotte walked along the street towards her car that she'd moved to allow them to park the van. She got in, hidden by the van, and waited for the black car to pass. She manoeuvred out of the spot and followed, leaving an exasperated-looking Seven standing on the path with his hands in the air.

The journey ended at the hospital. The nurse had parked in a staff bay, so Charlotte nipped into the space beside it and followed the woman into the building. There was going to come a point when Charlotte would look conspicuous and someone would notice her, so she kept back in case the nurse spun round. It didn't take long to find out where the woman was going. They'd reached a set of double doors, a plaque above it pronouncing it as THE HOME HELP SOCIETY. Charlotte hadn't known that such a place existed within a hospital, or maybe it was a new thing, but whatever it was, it confused her even more.

If Grace was going to be murdered, why had Mint risked hiring home help?

What the bloody hell was going on?

Charlotte's attention snagged on a framed set of photographs on the wall beside the double doors. She had a look to see if the nurse was on it, and there she was, Polly Wright, senior home help. Charlotte walked away from the doors in case she got spotted, making her way back through the hospital. In the car, she tossed her phone on the passenger seat and drove away. At the nearest McDonald's, she went through the drive-through and ordered a Big Mac and a coffee. Parked up, she ate while deep-diving into Polly's life on Facebook.

At the point where Charlotte had taken the last bite of her burger, she came upon a post that had the same photograph that had been in the summer house — Grace and her husband. Polly had written a post to go with it.

> Absolutely heartbroken to lose one of my clients this morning. Frank was an exceptional human being and leaves behind his much-loved wife, Grace. I was stunned to learn that he gifted some money to me because I cared for him for two years. What a gent! RIP Frank, until we meet again.

Charlotte's mind was all over the place. This changed things significantly. Had Grace been cared for by Polly in her home, too, and she was also after her money when the old woman died? Had she persuaded Grace to leave everything to her? Charlotte had the burning urge to go back and check on Grace, but instead she'd use the old payphone in the back of the betting shop down Salthurst Way.

Charlotte set off in the car, parking in the multi-storey near town. On the way to the bookies, she phoned Seven. "Where are you?"

"Waiting for you outside Mint's in the van. What the fuck's going on?"

"Go to the new flat. I'll meet you there in about half an hour and explain everything then."

"Fuck's sake, don't tell me you let that nurse see you following."

"It's fine, but I found out who she is and kind of know what's going on. There's no nephew or mate of Mint's, but he's still got to be involved because one, how the hell did the nurse get into the house to see Grace unless she had a key or one of the other residents let her in, and two, I didn't tell you what Grace said about having an estate agent round for dinner. His description was the same as Mint's."

"Why the fuck didn't you tell me?"

"Because you were all for letting the old girl die and taking a step back as if we didn't know about it. I can't do that."

"Don't do anything stupid…"

"Just go to the flat. I'll see you soon."

Charlotte ended the call and entered the bookies. Men sat on bar stools at a counter running down the side of the shop. They didn't pay her any mind, so she walked to the back and dialled nine-nine-nine. She poured everything out quickly, stating that an old woman was in danger, being kept in an attic. She gave the address then slammed the phone down, leaving the bookies with her chin to her chest and her eyes up, shaking from the stress of it all. Mint was going to suspect it was her or Seven, especially because they'd just moved out today, but he couldn't prove it, no more than she could prove the fact that he and Polly were involved in this up to their armpits, but if it meant Grace got saved, then it would go some way to assuaging Charlotte's guilt at stealing the jewellery.

How the fuck had her life come to this? One minute she'd been starting work at the solicitor's; there had been parties and the high life with her colleagues, booze and cigarettes, the occasional line of coke that had turned into something so much more. And now she was involved in some bitch intending to kill an old lady, possibly for money. Maybe Polly and Mint were together and they'd hatched a plan between them. Like he didn't earn enough money from selling drugs.

Charlotte drove to the new flat. She let herself in and found Seven sitting on the sofa he'd had in his old room. She was going to have to put a throw over it because it was so ugly, but it would do for now. She sat beside him and told him everything she'd learned, expecting him to have a go at her for calling the police, but he didn't.

"Right, if we get dragged into this because we lived at the house and just happened to move out today," he said, "then you'll admit to sitting with Grace because you felt sorry for her but not because Mint told you to. I'm telling you, that man is darker than we could ever imagine, he's got fingers in some serious pies, and I don't want to get brought into this bollocks when I told you to mind your own business and not phone the coppers."

"Fine, I'm happy to do that because I don't particularly want him on my arse anyway. I'll make out I don't know what he's talking about and that I had no intention of grassing him up. Think about it, though. We told him this morning that we were leaving, and he wasn't particularly bothered because he knows damn well that Grace is going to die tonight. I bet you any money there's a fake tenancy agreement that says he's renting to her. That would be how he gets away with someone entering the house to kill her with an overdose, he can say Grace gave them a spare key."

"But the police are going to ask questions as to why she's renting a shitty attic when she's got a perfectly lovely house to live in."

"He said something about making out she was distraught about losing her husband, remember? At least I'm sure that's what he said but I was high at the time."

"You didn't imagine it, I remember that as well. Okay, so now I'm worried that the police might poke into it so far that they check who made that phone call. Where did you do it?"

"In the bookies down Salthurst Way. You know what it's like down there; I doubt there's even CCTV. It's one of those shithole streets that people avoid if they can help it."

"You'd better hope that's true, plus that there's no CCTV inside the bookies."

"It's not like I've been in trouble with the police before and they can run my mug shot, is it."

"No, but they can plaster your fucking photo all over Facebook. Bet you didn't think of that, *did you?" He sat back, smug, arms folded.*

"I'll just have to pray that luck's on my side, won't I, and nothing like that happens. And if I do get found out, then I'll just hold my hands up and say it was me and I was scared of what would happen if the person keeping Grace in that room found me." She sounded convinced that it would work but didn't feel it. However, Seven didn't need to know that. "I'll order

pizza. We can eat it in between putting our things away."

Seven sat forward, his legs wide apart, hands dangling between his knees. "What the fuck have we become?"

"Good people, we're being good now, and if we keep being good then karma won't come to get us."

All she could do was pray that was true.

Chapter Twelve

George had a bad feeling in his gut about this Mint bloke. Ever since he'd been caught peddling drugs, he'd become a thorn in their side. Several warnings had been issued from the watchers on the streets, all of them ignored by Mint until George had given the order to stab the fucker. And now look, he was off out again tonight as if a blade hadn't parted his skin.

"Next time, I'll give the order for a nine-inch knife. Maybe *then* he'll listen," he muttered to himself as Greg drove around the River Walk estate. "I think we've been very fair so far, don't you?"

"Yeah, especially when we know so much about him now. There's a lot to unpack with regards to him, and not many leaders would allow someone like that to stay on their Estate if they're not going to comply with the rules. If he doesn't listen after the nine-incher then we get rid. Dump him back on the Greaves Estate and tell Nathaniel he can deal with him—and if he doesn't, then we call an emergency leader meeting to report him."

"I like it when we have a plan. What I don't like is waiting for a message to come through to say Mint's left one of the houses in Anchor Avenue or he's gone back home."

"He might not be in Anchor."

"I *know*, I said that earlier when Moody was here, which is why we're driving round at bastard o'clock trying to spot him, shit for brains."

Greg laughed. "Why do you let me wind you up?"

"I try not to, but sometimes you're so irritating that I can't help it."

Ralph stuck his head between the seats.

"Here's the referee," Greg said.

George fussed the dog under the chin. "That's right, it's me you need to protect. I'm your master."

"He's only best friends with you because you feed him."

"No, he's best friends with me because he loves me the most."

"What if I told you he's best friends with me every time you leave the room?"

George scoffed. "You're just a poor substitute. He's all over me again when I come back in."

"Holding a treat. You've bribed him to love you more. Do you need to go and see Vic for therapy?"

George was about to flip his lid but at the last second realised Greg was winding him up again. "You're lucky I don't punch your fucking lights out, bruv."

Greg slowed to let someone in a dark hoodie cross the road. "Is that him?"

"I can't see properly until we go closer."

Greg beeped the horn, and the person jumped a mile, spinning round to stare at the van. A kid, no more than fifteen, her eyes wide, the blonde hair either side of her cheeks bright in the headlights. She slapped her hand to her heart, gave them a scowl, then ran off towards a high-rise.

"You scared the poor little cow," George said.

"I didn't mean to. The clothing matched Mint's description, not to mention she's the same height and build."

"Everyone wears those fucking hoodies these days."

"Us included."

They drove on, George getting bored with people-spotting. He reckoned it was about the right time to tell Greg something he'd kept from him for the past four hours. He'd been asked to keep it a secret by Greg's ex, Ineke Meijer. George couldn't stand the bitch once he'd got to know her, and he'd been glad when the pair had split up, but he wasn't looking forward to the bollocking he was going to get.

"Um, I've got something to tell you."

Greg sighed. "Fuck, the way you said that, it sounds like I'm not going to be happy. What have you done this time?"

"I kept a secret for someone and I'm telling you now because I was told I could around about this time."

"What are you on about?"

"Ineke."

"What about her?"

"She texted me to give us notice that she's leaving the flat." George waited for the inevitable fallout, prepared to apologise, which he should anyway because he'd promised not to keep anything from his brother, but in this case he'd thought it was the best way forward.

"When?" Greg asked.

"When did she text me or when is she leaving?"

"Jesus, when is she *leaving*?"

Here was where the bomb would hit hardest if Greg had been lying all this time and he still had feelings for the woman.

"She's already left," George said.

"What? How long have you known about this?"

"Four hours."

"Where's she gone?"

"She didn't say, but I do know it isn't London." And thank God for that. Ever since those two had parted ways, George had hated having to see her if she had something she needed to tell them to their faces regarding their investments, ones she'd worked on for them. She'd handed all that over earlier, with instructions for the next person they employed to deal with it, and the first thing he'd done was change the passwords on all the online portals. He really didn't need her stealing their money with him not knowing where to find her so he could cut her fucking face off.

Greg gripped the steering wheel. "How is she going to afford to live without our help?"

"You mean us paying her and letting her live rent-free in one of our flats?"

"Yes."

"So you still care about her then."

Greg tutted. "I care about *all* of our residents—well, not the pricks, but you know what I mean."

Here was another potential bombshell. And George really should have spoken to Greg about this, considering it involved a lot of money. "To answer your question, she asked for a loan."

"How much?"

"Thirty grand."

"Did you give it to her?"

"Of course I did, and it wasn't a loan."

"You paid her off so she doesn't come back."

George cringed. "That's one way of looking at it."

"Good."

George's eyebrows scooted up. He hadn't expected that response. "She said she couldn't stay around here anymore, that she'd basically woken up and realised she was taking the piss by letting us fund her living expenses and university course when she was no longer seeing you. She said she needs to earn money and get on by herself."

"With thirty grand. That's hardly going to be difficult for her, is it, when she's got a nest egg sitting under her. Fucking hell, she really does take the biscuit. Anyway, thanks for helping her, but you didn't need to keep it quiet until she'd actually left London, which is what I assume you did. What did you both think, that if I knew about it I'd try and stop her from going? Not likely."

"Ineke said you wouldn't go after her, she's well aware of the score, clearly, but I wasn't so sure."

"You know me better than anyone, so why the fuck weren't you sure? I *told* you I was done with her. It was an infatuation, nothing more. Women are trouble, we both know we're not destined to be with one long-term."

George didn't see the point in bleating on with this subject anymore. "How long are we going drive around looking for this cunt?"

"Another hour, although I'll stop over here because it sounds like Ralph's whining for a wee."

They got out of the van, George suspecting that Greg needed a bit of fresh air to get his head around the latest news. Maybe he was celebrating Ineke actually leaving, who knew, but George was. Ralph ran around in circles on a stretch of green between houses, snorting and snuffling in his excitement. A few people walked by on their way home from the boozer up the road, and Ralph bounded over to them for a sniff and a stroke.

"Sorry about him," George called. "He goes a bit over the top but won't hurt you."

Ralph rolled onto his back for a tummy rub, and after receiving one from a man in corduroy trousers with a seriously long combover, the silly dog ran to sniff the grass farther away. He finally did a wee, and they all got back in the van.

"Do you reckon Mint's got a case of blue balls, and that's why he tried to get a woman at the parlour?" George asked.

Greg pulled away from the kerb. "He probably just wants a shag because he hasn't had one in a long time. He likely used his dad's name because he suspected a check would be done and the fact that he's been in the nick would come up. You don't hear about the parlour unless you know someone who's used it, so he must have learned about it by word of mouth, especially if he walked into The Angel and went straight down the corridor."

Lisa, the manager, had forwarded them CCTV footage.

"I wonder if his father told him we nipped round there to ask him which of the women he wanted to get his leg over with?" George pondered. "Did you see his face? Outrage. I thought he was going to have a heart attack."

"What did you think about what Nathanial said?"

"What bit?"

"That Mint grew up thinking he didn't have a dad, and it was well known to a fair few people that it was Timmons who owned the corner shop, and the bloke had been keeping an eye on Mint for years but had never stepped forward to help raise him."

"No different to our father. Ron watched us growing up, he even employed us as his bully boys, for fuck's sake, yet he never said a word. Mint was luckier than us because he didn't have a surrogate father who beat the shit out of him—not that we know of anyway. Better to have no dad than a man like Richard. Anyway, let's not talk about those two, or I'll end up getting in a bad mood."

They went down another few streets.

"I'm calling it," Greg said.

George agreed. "Let's go home. Tomorrow's another day."

Chapter Thirteen

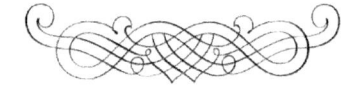

Mint stood in the back garden between two bushes. One had yellow flowers on it. They stank like cheap perfume, the scent getting right in his throat. He should have moved away from them ages ago—he'd spent the past five minutes trying not to cough. He could do with a nice cup of tea, but he doubted Charlotte would be in a receptive mood if she caught him. She'd ring the police or the twins.

He'd hung around for the lights to go off, and when they had he'd waited twenty minutes more. It was about time he got a shift on. Just a little something to show her he was the one in charge. It was a step farther than he'd gone in the past, and he was seriously pushing his luck, but he hadn't liked the way Charlotte had treated him in the Red Lion, as if he wasn't someone she wanted to be seen with and he wasn't good enough for her.

He sidled along with the bushes at his back, then went up the side, keeping close to the high wooden fence. He paused at the gate, like he had when he'd come into the garden, to see if a security light flashed on. Nothing. At the back door, he turned the handle on the off chance the door would open, but it remained shut. Stupid of him to have thought she wouldn't have locked up, especially knowing that he was out and about again. She wasn't dumb enough to think that him being friendly with her earlier meant they were actually friends. She'd always be on her guard when it came to him, and he couldn't really blame her.

He took a pick out of his pocket and inserted it into the lock, jiggling it this way and that until a clunk sounded to let him know he'd been successful. He waited in the darkness for a moment or two, to see if she came to investigate the noise, but she must be asleep; no lights popped on indoors to seep around the closed curtains, ones she'd drawn about half an hour ago. She hadn't even stared down into the garden when she'd done it, get you'd think a woman would be security conscious when she lived alone.

Assuming she lived alone. If she didn't, then he had to be on his guard in case some bloke came bounding along to sort him out.

Mint let himself in, closing the door behind him, standing there stock-still, listening. Only the sound of his breathing broke the silence, and then his footsteps as he trod carefully through the living room and out into a long, carpeted hallway with a front door at the end. There were two doors on one side, three on the other; a kitchen, three bedrooms, and a bathroom, he presumed. He was going to have to check all of them; he didn't know which one she'd gone into or even if she'd gone out via the front. It would be easier if she'd done the latter, at least then he could have a good nose around and get his bearings, then go and wait for her in her bedroom until she came back.

He wasn't sure if he was going to fuck her yet or just do the business over her while she slept. Even though he'd be using his hand, it would still be more exciting to have a woman present.

The first two doors on the left were a bathroom and kitchen, both spotlessly tidy, and the first on the right was a room with a single bed in it—and a lot of toys in a row of wicker baskets down one wall. Blue walls, blue duvet cover and curtains. She had a son? He inched along to the next door, presented with much the same, except this one was done out in red. Another boy? Where was the father? She hadn't mentioned one, but then they weren't exactly bosom buddies yet, were they.

He leaned on the wall between the rooms to take in the new information. Kids. While he'd been festering away in prison, she'd resumed her life by having a relationship and giving birth to two children, and he'd bet she'd never given him a second thought either.

But why should she?

He didn't know, but it still bugged him that she'd been free and he hadn't. Not that she'd done anything wrong except know the old lady was going to be killed, but he justified his antagonism towards her because at the time he'd thought she'd phoned the police about him and the garage full of drugs. She'd cleared up the fact that it hadn't been her, but his resentment still remained. Maybe it was going to take time for him to stop thinking of her as the enemy. To be fair, if she tidied herself up a bit she wouldn't be half bad, and he could use her, live here until he got himself sorted.

But if you fuck her after breaking into her flat, she's not likely to want to tidy herself up for you, is she.

Where were the children now? Had they been taken away from her? She looked the sort who social services would be interested in—*that* was how much she'd changed in appearance—so it wouldn't be any wonder that those bedrooms stood empty. What the hell had gone on that things had come to this?

He pushed off the wall, took a steadying breath, and slowly opened the last door. A night light glowed in the corner—was she afraid of the dark?—and he could make out the lump of her in the bed. She was under a white quilt, there for the taking if he wanted to indulge, and while his mind kept telling him she wasn't his type, his dick kept saying it didn't matter because any hole would do so long as it was clean. He had a condom in his pocket.

He crept in, making it to the side of her bed without creating any noise, although he swore his breathing sounded laboured and far too loud. Every little thing seemed to be amplified; even the way his clothing shifted when he moved. Was she really awake, pretending to be asleep in the hope he'd go away? Had she already phoned the police? Was it better that he fucked off now instead of praying he didn't get caught?

Just a minute or so more, and if he hadn't made his mind up by then, he was going to have to leave and find someone else.

She lay on her side, a standing fan blowing her hair from the other side of the bed, the quilt tucked beneath her chin, despite this being summer and the air too warm. The light only illuminated the top half of the bed, and *his* top half should she open her eyes and see him, so he stepped back to just outside the glow so he'd be a shadowy figure.

He wanted to go closer, to peel the quilt away and give her body a good once-over from head to toe, asking himself one last time whether he could look at the mantel while poking the fireplace or whether he'd have to shut his eyes. She was still pretty, he'd give her that, but she'd changed her lovely hair, dying it darker. She must also dye her eyebrows as they matched.

He knelt, much more comfortable now to study her, although really it was only her face and hair he got a good look at. But then she threw the bedding off, rolling onto her back, exposing her pyjama-covered body. Pyjamas, in this weather? The air from the fans stirred the fabric of her top, the hem just above her belly button. He watched it fluttering, waiting for her to wake up at the irritation, but her breathing deepened.

He stood and walked into the light, the toes of his trainers going beneath the divan, his shins and knees touching the mattress. He bent so his face was millimetres away from hers, and as she breathed out, he breathed in. Tasted her.

She opened her eyes.

And screamed.

Chapter Fourteen

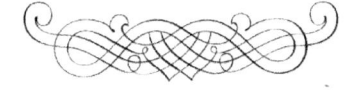

Two months had passed since they'd moved into the flat. Two months of Charlotte shitting herself thinking the police were going to catch up with her again at some point. Every time she logged on to Facebook she was paranoid her face would pop up once she was scrolling, the local police page appealing for anyone to come forward if they 'know this woman'. It

was wreaking havoc with her nerves, but at least Grace wasn't dead.

It had made the news, the headline screaming: OLD WOMAN MURDER PLOT FOILED. It sounded so old-fashioned, but everyone was lapping it up. There was even a Facebook page dedicated to Grace, where people discussed the nurse, Polly, and how you couldn't even trust someone who worked in a hospital, and then there stemmed a discussion about not trusting nurses anyway, because there were baby deaths and all sorts going on behind the scenes, staff behaving badly.

Charlotte had scoured them all to try and find out whether her involvement had been discovered, but why would she find that out online first rather than the police contacting her? She was being paranoid, but who could blame her when she'd been willing to allow Grace to die at one point, all for a couple of hundred quid a pop to sit with her so she could expand her savings pot. When Charlotte thought about it that way, she was disgusted with herself. It was as if she'd been a different person when it had all gone on. She no longer took coke, she had about ten cigarettes a week, and she allowed herself a couple of drinks if she went out with her colleagues instead of downing a bottle of wine to herself and rolling home pissed as a fart.

She had to be so careful now, couldn't allow herself to slip up.

Seven had withdrawn from her. They barely spoke if they were in the kitchen or living room at the same time, and maybe that was for the best. He was trying hard to become a better person, too, and with their shared secrets it was possibly proving difficult for him to push that side of himself into the past where it belonged. Strange that he was maybe struggling, because as the coke-sniffing Seven, he hadn't been bothered about Grace at all and what would become of her. Now, when the police had got involved, having spoken to them two days after they'd moved to the flat, he had suddenly grown a conscience. Or maybe that was a fear of being arrested as part of a murder plot.

So far, Charlotte had successfully pulled the wool over the eyes of the police, but she'd convinced herself that might not last for long. Because of the worry of her DNA being found in the attic room, she'd admitted to sitting with Grace but only because she knew an old lady lived up there and she felt sorry for her. She said she'd carried on the ruse that she was a carer because she thought Grace possibly suffered from dementia and she didn't want to upset her. According to a few articles, Mint had been spoken to as a person of interest but was let go shortly after Polly admitted she'd been visiting Grace at her house after Frank had died, trying to get her to change her will, and when she hadn't, she'd forged her signature on a new one, sent it to Grace's solicitor, and then played the long game.

A year after continuing to visit Grace in Prophet Gardens, and with no inkling from Grace that she was aware the will had changed, Polly had got bored of waiting so had arranged for Grace to be taken to the attic. The plan was for Grace to overdose after writing a letter stating how much she missed Frank.

Life had gone on, Charlotte's once again looking to the outsider that nothing was amiss, when in fact she was a boiling mass of anxiety inside. She kept expecting the police to ask to speak to her again, for Grace to perhaps remember a conversation she may have overheard when Charlotte wasn't there, maybe Mint discussing the woman who lived on the second floor who was paid to sit with her.

Many times Charlotte contemplated running away. For good, changing her name and everything, not even speaking to her parents. If she disappeared then all this would go away. She could dye her hair, put on some weight, get herself some glasses. It wouldn't take much to change her, but what would she do for work? She'd lose all of her credentials as Charlotte, unless she retrained in the new name. Was that how these things worked? Could she still be tracked if she used deed poll?

She sighed, walking into the flat from work, out of sorts and needing something, anything to take away this horrible feeling inside her. Seven sat on the sofa watching telly, biting his fingernail. He was likely itching for a fix, and she sympathised with how hard it was to remain clean.

"Do you want to go to the pub for dinner and a drink, my treat?" she asked.

"Can do."

"Well, you could at least pretend *you're excited. Christ." She dropped her bag on the coffee table and went into her room to get changed out of her skirt suit into some jeans and a lightweight jumper. She refreshed her makeup and brushed her hair, going back to the living room and scowling at Seven who hadn't moved an inch. "Are you coming then or what?"*

He got up and followed her into the hallway, stuffing his feet in his trainers and taking his coat from the hook on the wall. He put it on, the material drowning him.

"Is it the stress of all the Grace business or the lack of coke that's making you look so gaunt?" she asked, one hand on the Yale lock ready to open the door.

"Like you care."

"I wouldn't have asked if I didn't care."

"I just don't feel like eating, all right?"

"So we're going to go out for a meal and you're not going to order anything."

"I didn't say that…what I meant was that I don't like cooking so half the time I don't bother."

"If you put some money towards the food shop then I'll cook for you every evening, but I'm not doing it unless you pay up."

"Fine."

She opened the door and headed for the communal front door, hauling it wide and stopping short, staring down at the top step in a set of four that led down to the pavement. She slapped her hand to her mouth at the sight of the blood, at the lips drawn back, exposing the tiny teeth. She let out a squeak and bent to pick the cat up, but Seven's warning stopped her.

"Leave it. Looks like his owner's coming home now," he said.

Charlotte glanced up.

The woman rushed along, her face a picture of misery as she spotted her animal on the step. "Oh God, no…"

"I'm so sorry," Charlotte said. "We literally just opened the door and found it here."

The woman went down on her knees and scooped the animal up, crying her eyes out. Charlotte stepped around her and went down the stairs, guilt giving her a good poke for seeming so uncaring, but that cat's throat had been slit, that was no accidental death, and she didn't want to be anywhere near it until she got her head around what the implications might mean.

"Do you want me to call someone?" Seven asked the neighbour.

At least one of them was doing the right thing.

She got up and rushed inside.

Seven closed the door, stared down at the blood on the step, and shook his head. "Maybe we ought to clean that so she doesn't see it next time she comes out. A reminder, you know—could be painful."

Charlotte felt like a bitch, but she didn't offer to do it. She always had to do everything. She waited for him to go inside and get a bucket of bleach water and clean the step. He was a good bloke deep down, he'd just got messed up the same as she had, the coke fucking with his brain. He went inside to take the bucket back, then joined her on the pavement.

The walk to the pub was made in silence, the smell of bleach coming off him reminding her of swimming pools and happier times as a child. She wasn't sure why she'd reacted so coldly with the cat and its owner — maybe she had enough worries of her own that she couldn't take on anyone else's. Or maybe she was just a selfish cow with no empathy.

She needed to do better.

The pub was packed when they entered, and it annoyed her having to squish past people who wouldn't move out of the way. She finally made it to the bar, looking through to the other side where the restaurant was, happy it wasn't as busy there. She requested a table for two and was told to go next door, where they were shown to a corner. Charlotte stared at the menu without taking in the words, her mind on her behaviour as they'd left the flat. It was really bothering her that she hadn't offered help like Seven had.

They ordered pie and chips each with a boat of gravy, and she splashed out on a bottle of wine for them to share. Seven looked like he needed something to take the edge off, and she could do with the same. She wasn't sure what to talk to him about now that their shared love of coke no longer existed — well, it did, they still loved it but had chosen not to take it.

"Are you sure you're okay living with me?" she asked after their silent dinner was over and they were two glasses of wine in. "I always feel like I've done something wrong."

"You did, you went to the bloody police."

"You weren't bothered about it at the time. I expected you to have a go at me, and you didn't. I don't understand how letting the old woman die would be better than stopping her murder. We're out the other side of whatever deluded mess we got our brains into with the drugs, and surely you can see it wasn't a good thing to let someone kill her."

"I get that, yeah, but it's just…look, my life is really shit without coke. I'm depressed, nothing makes me smile anymore."

"Maybe you need therapy."

"Fuck off."

"I wasn't taking the piss, I'm serious."

He stared out of the window, his face paling, and he downed the rest of his wine in one go, giving a little shudder after. She stared over her shoulder to see what had bothered him.

Mint walked across the car park towards the pub door.

Fuck.

Since when did he know where they drank? He'd never mentioned it before when they'd lived in his house, but then why would he? Or maybe he'd only recently found out. Or he could just be coming here for a drink. Charlotte peered around at the other customers. Had someone grassed them up and told him where they were? She cursed herself now for even coming here. They'd been so used to it because of living up the road at Mint's, but they should have been sensible and found a new pub by the flat.

She stared over in the direction of the open door. There he was, looking round like he was searching for someone. It didn't take long before his attention landed on them.

"Oh God," Seven muttered.

"He's not going to help us, is he," Charlotte muttered back. "I wonder what the fuck Mint wants. He must know from being interviewed by the police that we never said anything about that bloody murder plot."

"He might not even be here for us."

"Er, I think you'll find he is."

Mint came storming over and plonked himself on the spare seat at their table. "Have you found another dealer or what?"

So that was what he wanted to talk to them about? Drugs? Not an old lady's death?

"We're both clean now," Charlotte said. "New flat, new life."

"Blimey, never thought I'd see the day." *Mint narrowed his eyes at her and leaned forward, probably so his voice wouldn't be overheard, which meant he might say something she didn't want to hear. "I wanted to say cheers about not getting me in the shit."*

"In the shit for what?" she asked.

Mint smiled. "Ah, I like what you did there, pretending you didn't know anything about it, same as you told the police."

"I didn't want to get dragged into all that bullshit along with that nurse, just because I sat with the old dear for a few nights—and that's all it amounted to, me sitting with her and you renting the room to Polly. Stick with that story, and everything will be fine."

Mint nodded, mulling over her words. "It sounds simple when you put it like that, but Polly's now trying to get me drawn into it, as if I was the one who made the plan in the first place, when all I did was go to Grace's bloody house and be an estate agent."

"Let's not forget you allowed an old lady to be stashed up in your attic. I mean, how did she even go to the toilet?"

Mint raised his hands, palms facing her. "Don't fucking ask me, I've got no idea. I barely went in that room."

Charlotte remembered something, and she wasn't going to let him get away with sweeping some of his actions under the carpet. Besides, if he knew she'd read a lot more into things and that he could actually end up going to prison if she opened her mouth, then maybe they could come to some agreement that he never spoke to them again. She didn't need him breathing down her neck.

"You said you were an estate agent. It was you who went to Grace's house with a bottle of champagne and two glasses, wasn't it. You drugged her and took her to the attic."

Mint's mouth dropped open. "Where the fuck did you hear that load of rubbish?"

She could grass Grace up and say it was her but she didn't want to put the old dear in any danger. The online newspapers said she'd gone into some assisted-living place where nurses were there around the clock—Charlotte assumed she had some kind of flat where she could be independent but press a button if she wanted company or whatever.

"Haven't you read the news today?" Charlotte asked. "Polly's been talking again."

Mint blinked. "You what?"

"Like I just said, Polly's been talking. It's looking more and more likely that you're going to be spoken to again, and if you want to keep yourself out of prison with regards to me and Seven, then I suggest you don't come and speak to us, you leave us alone, because we don't want anything to do with it. Or…"

He scraped his chair back and stood, planting his hands on the table and leaning close to her face. "Don't you threaten me…"

"I'm not threatening. All I'm doing is telling you to leave me and my mate out of this."

"Yeah, well, the threat should come the other way, from my direction. It's you two who need to keep your mouths shut. If you don't, then I'm going to get even more catty."

He over-pronounced that last word, and Charlotte's stomach rolled over. Had he killed that bloody cat? Did he know where they lived now? She hadn't had time to school her features so he wouldn't know how much he'd bothered her, and he caught her expression of shock. Smirking, he pushed off the table and sauntered towards the door, pausing as though contemplating whether to have a drink or not, then thinking better of it and walking out. Charlotte watched him through the window until he'd got in a car and driven off.

"What did you do that for?" Seven whispered.

She turned to him. He didn't look well. "Do what?"

"Making out that I'm in agreement with you about threatening him. You said 'me and my mate'. I didn't give you permission to speak for me."

She stared at him in shock. "Hang on a minute, if I remember rightly, you're the one who told me it was okay to be involved in killing an old granny, and now that the shit's hit the fan, you want nothing to do with it, yet you were quite happy for me to earn the money for sitting with her so we could get the fuck out of that house. Double standards much?"

She did the same as Mint and walked out, not giving a fuck that she'd left almost half a bottle of wine. Let Seven drink himself silly, getting all depressed. It was doing her head in, his down moods. They were bringing **her** *down, too, and she didn't know how much longer she could hack it. The problem was, all three of them were worried about what the other was going to do. Seven knew she'd told the police about Grace, and for all he knew she could ring them again and tell them that Seven had known all about it. But she wouldn't, because then he'd tell the police that* **she'd** *known about it.*

Fucking hell, what a mess. She wished she hadn't phoned them and instead taken Grace from the house when they'd driven to the flat after cleaning their rooms. When she thought about it logically, what kind of person was she to leave the old woman in the attic, knowing the murder would be soon because Seven had heard the conversation through the ceiling?

She ought to be bloody ashamed of herself, and she was, but selfishly she worried that she'd have to stick with Seven for the rest of her life. They'd be forced friends because of the secret. Then there was Mint, who now seemed to know where they lived if his 'catty' comment was anything to go by—and that was too big of a coincidence for her to brush it off. What a sick bastard, doing that to an animal, and that poor neighbour was devastated. There hadn't been enough blood on the step for the killing to have happened there, so what had he done, kidnapped the bloody thing, taken it away, then done the deed and returned it?

She stormed home, to a flat that felt like an uncomfortable prison, angry that doing the right thing had turned out to be such a pain in the arse.

Chapter Fifteen

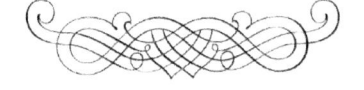

Sharon couldn't believe what the fuck she was seeing. Mint loomed so close to her. She blinked, thinking she was dreaming, but then his breath landed on her mouth, hot and horrible. She went to scream again, taking a deep breath, but he reared back and slapped her face. She registered he had a glove on, possibly leather from the feel of it against her skin. She kicked out to the side where he stood, her shin brushing his thighs, then she quickly rolled onto her side and drove one of her knees into one of his. He bent double from where she'd caught a glancing blow to his cock with the movement, staggering back, giving her enough time to jump out of bed. She grabbed a heavy brass ornament from the bedside cabinet and brandished it, reaching for her phone, too.

This had gone too far now. She was going to have to confess all to the twins.

His heavy breathing gave her the willies.

"Come anywhere near me again and you'll find this Eiffel Tower embedded in your head," she warned.

She advanced on him, forcing him out of the room in reverse. She was at a disadvantage in the hallway now that there was no light, but her eyes quickly adjusted. He was backing into the living room; he'd probably entered that way. Fucking hell, had she forgotten to lock the patio doors before she'd gone to bed?

"Where do you think you're going?" She smiled as he made it to the exit. "Sit the fuck down, because you need to wait for the twins."

His laugh grated on her last nerve. "The twins? Fuck right off, you stupid bint."

One-handed, she managed to bring her screen alive and, bouncing between staring at him and her phone while she navigated to her contact list, she watched him step out into the garden.

"What do you even *want*?" she asked. "I thought we'd made a deal."

"I wanted something from you, but I changed my mind."

She had a feeling she knew what he wanted. "So you were going to rape me?"

"I wouldn't call it something as strong as that."

He darted into the darkness, the sound of the gate clattering shut behind him loud in the night. With the ornament still raised and her thumb connecting with the icon named GG, she chased after him, the ground biting into her bare feet. She dashed along to where she thought he'd have gone, to the back of the flats, and the sound of an engine confirmed she'd chosen the right direction.

"Sharon?"

She quickly put the phone to her ear. "Yes, I need help."

"Calm down, you're all out of breath," George said.

"Because I'm running after some bastard who was in my flat." She reached the street, only to find red taillights greeting her. "Shit, he's gone."

"Who was it?"

"Someone I used to know."

"Who?"

"He goes by the name of Mint."

"*That* fucker? We've been out looking for him. How…?"

"It's a long story."

"Go home, stick the kettle on, and we'll be there in a minute."

Sharon trudged home, the ornament heavy now the adrenaline had buggered off. She'd held the weapon up no problem when she'd been hyped up on fear, but she had the insane urge to lie on the pavement and never get up again. She pushed herself forward, a dose of anxiety coming out to play at the thought of having to tell George and Greg the truth.

She walked into her garden and closed the gate, then the worry slammed into her that she'd left it open, and the patio door, and someone could be in her flat right now, rummaging through her things with a view to stealing them. She lifted the ornament again and entered the living room, shut the patio door, and prowled around her home, ready to swing out in self-defence if she had to. The adrenaline was back, shooting through her veins until she felt sick with it.

No one else was there.

She locked up, putting the Eiffel Tower on the sideboard in the living room and her phone in the pocket of her pyjama top. She went into the kitchen to fill the kettle with water and put it on to boil. She lit a cigarette—in her opinion, the encounter with Mint warranted one—and waited for the sound of a vehicle out the front.

It didn't take long, the rumble louder than it would be in the day, and she peeked out of the window. The twins were getting out of a van, their dog leaping out after them. All three of them walked towards the front door. She ran the tap, putting the cigarette under the stream. It sizzled, the orange end going out, and she quickly wrapped a square of kitchen roll around it then put it in the bin. She opened the door, stepping back to allow them to come in. Ralph licked her fingers on the way past, and for some reason it made her want to cry.

"What the fuck, Sharon," George said, his voice carrying from the kitchen where he'd gone.

She followed Greg in there. "Sorry, but I had no one else to ring."

She was about to sort the drinks, but Greg stood at the worktop waving her away, so she sat at the table opposite George. This was it, something she'd vowed never to tell anyone, but Mint had to be stopped.

"I've been lying by omission," she said.

"How come?" George asked.

"Think of it like me putting myself in witness protection except I did all the name-changing and whatever myself."

"You were hiding from Mint?"

"Yes, me and my friend were."

"Who's that?"

"His name's Seven."

"Fuck me, really?"

"I'm not prepared to tell you what his real name is, I promised I'd keep it a secret. Mint reckons it was just a coincidence that he was outside the Shiny Fork, but I don't know whether to believe him or not."

"So what happened?" Greg asked, bringing the cups over and sitting at the table with them. "Got any biscuits?"

"In that tin over there, on the microwave."

Greg got up to get them, sitting again and smiling at the contents of the tin, taking out a bourbon and biting into it. Sharon couldn't stand those bloody things, but the kids loved dipping them in Nutella.

Ralph came to sit on her feet, as if he knew she needed some comfort. As she stroked his head, she threw herself into the story, leaving out the bits that made her look bad—like stealing the jewellery. It really didn't sound so awful now so many years had passed, that she'd sat with an old lady and went to her house to feed a bird that had ended up dead, but the bit that she really embellished was Mint leaving the cat on the doorstep and everything that had happened after that, before she and Seven had managed to get away.

"So he's got a beef with you because he spent all that time in prison thinking you'd grassed him up. As you've just said, it *was* you, and you did the right thing in telling him it wasn't, but from what I can gather, if he came here tonight then it means he still doesn't believe you, even though he said he did."

"He was here for something else." She shuddered and explained waking up, staring straight into Mint's eyes.

"Dirty fucking bastard," Greg said. "He was after a bird at The Angel, too. There are so many things we want to kill him for. What started off as some pleb selling drugs on our patch has turned into so much more."

"What are you going to do?" Sharon asked.

"Kill him, otherwise he's never going to leave you alone."

She nodded absently. "You know he's going to lie, don't you, when you ask him questions about Grace and my involvement."

"Of course he is, men like him always do."

"He wheedled his way out of it with the police, even though Polly stopped protecting him and swore blind he was a part of it all."

"But he served time anyway," George said, "so that's something, even if it was for drugs instead."

Sharon told them about having to make the decision to walk away from her life completely, cutting off her parents for their own safety.

"Why, was Mint a threat even from inside?" George asked.

"I wasn't sure so thought it best to be on the safe side. So after Mint resurfaced, I went back to the old Estate; Seven wanted to meet once he knew Mint was back on the scene, and after Seven said he was moving abroad, I went to the shop. The bloke who owns it said my mum had been in, and she always talks about me, and I realised how horrible it must have been for her, how it still is, for me to have told her that I needed space and didn't want anything to do with them anymore. I did tell them they hadn't done anything wrong, that it was all to do with me and how I felt, but now I'm a mother, I can see how she'd have tormented herself, and I feel rotten as fuck. But I can't take it back, all the years I stayed away and all the feelings she's been through, and my dad, and I'll feel guilty about that for the rest of my life."

"You could talk to her, on the phone," George suggested. "Tell her you were actually put into witness protection. She doesn't need to know whether you were or not. What's one more lie? You could make out you weren't allowed to say anything at the time because it was too dangerous and you knew she'd worry even more if she knew someone was after you."

"What the hell would I say had happened?"

"You witnessed a crime. Or if you don't think you can handle it, we can go round there for you and make something up."

"Yeah, maybe it's best that you do it. I've made such a mess of everything. Even when I got away, I couldn't even keep the father of my children."

"That's on him if his dick was wandering."

"I'd let myself go, that was the problem. I got comfortable because I felt safe."

George reached out and placed his hand on hers. "Stop beating yourself up. We know where Mint's staying, so we'll go round there now."

"Do I need to do anything?"

"Not unless you want to watch me kill him." George stood. "If you don't fancy that, then I suggest you go back to bed."

She nodded. Saw them out the front and waited until they'd driven away before she closed the door and locked it. There had been no reprimand about lying, about being a completely different person to who she really was. About telling them she struggled on her own as her parents had disowned her, when in fact, it had been the other way around. It was as if all that mattered to them was teaching Mint a lesson for what he'd done.

But maybe the chastisement would come later.

She walked into her bedroom and got beneath the covers, curling herself up in the foetal position, her phone clutched in her hand. She'd only feel safe when it beeped with a message to tell her that Mint had been found. In the meantime, she'd stay awake, staring at the wall.

Chapter Sixteen

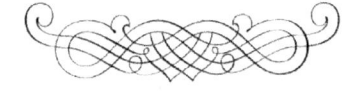

Standing on his threshold, Mr Timmons stared at George and Greg. "What the bloody hell do you two want *now*?"

"We'd like a word with you about your son."

"What about him?"

"It's best done indoors, don't you think? Or is he in there, hiding?"

"I haven't seen him for hours. He left ages ago after coming here for a visit."

"Then you won't mind if we step inside and take a look, will you."

The old man tutted and moved out of the way, pressing his back against the hallway wall to give them room to go past. Ralph shot inside and disappeared into one of the rooms. As was usually their way, Greg took downstairs while George went up. A quick scoot into all the bedrooms and the bathroom, even checking under the beds, and it was clear Mint wasn't there. George went down and found Greg in the back garden, his backside sticking out of a shed. Ralph cocked his leg against a bush.

Mr Timmons shuffled out after George, joining him on the patio. "I don't know what you expect to find, because I told you he wasn't here."

Greg came out of the shed, shut the door, and twisted a little black latch so it kept it closed. They congregated in the kitchen, Timmons filling the kettle and getting out some sachets of Horlicks.

"Not for us, thanks," Greg said from his seat at the table. "What can you tell us about your son? The type of person he is."

"Well, he's my boy, so what do you expect me to say?"

Greg sighed and looked at George who was in the process of parking his arse. "Let me make this easier, Mr Timmons. We're fully aware that you weren't in your son's life, as such, while he was growing up. You were there as the bloke in the corner shop but not as his dad. So from an outsider's point of view, which you clearly were, what did you make of him?"

Timmons ripped off the top of a sachet and tipped the powder into a cup he'd taken off the draining board. He collected a spoon and poured hot water, staring for a while, clearly thinking about how to answer. He carried his drink over and sat between George and Greg.

"From what I could gather, Minty was a bit of a sod for his mother as he was growing up. Didn't behave, didn't listen, that kind of thing. When he got older, I heard he was into drugs—not taking them but selling them, and I knew the only way to get him to stop was by telling Greaves about it, seeing as it was his Estate that it was happening on, but I couldn't do it, I couldn't grass up my own kid. So I turned a blind eye."

"Did you hear about his involvement with some woman called Polly regarding a murder plot to kill an old lady named Grace?"

"I remember it being in the news, yes, and thank God I'd moved over here by that point so I could distance myself. By all accounts he didn't do anything, or there was no proof anyway, and I asked him outright myself. He denied it, said he was just an estate agent, and I know he was, but it doesn't mean he wasn't involved."

"Do you think he was?"

"Like I told you, I didn't want to grass my son up, and that hasn't changed."

"Do you think he's capable of killing a cat and leaving it on a doorstep to frighten someone?"

"*What*? I should bloody well hope not, but you just don't know what these drug types get up to, do you?"

"How come you let him come here to see you?"

"He's got nowhere to go. His wife changed the bloody locks while he was in the nick." Timmons blew on his Horlicks and then sipped. "Shit, that's still too hot. What's he done? Why are you here?"

"He broke into one of our resident's homes this evening. Went into her bedroom while she slept. You can imagine what he had in mind, but she woke up and chased him out."

"Are you suggesting he was going to rape her?"

"Why, is this where you tell us he wouldn't do any such thing?"

Timmons stared at his drink. "The truth is, I don't actually know what he's capable of."

"Where is he?"

"I swear to you, I don't know."

George nodded. He believed him.

Chapter Seventeen

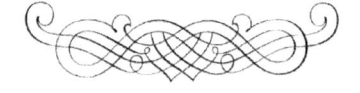

The second gift on the doorstep was a manky syringe that appeared to be full of blood and not heroin. Beside it, held down beneath a big grey pebble, a newspaper clipping of Grace's story. Mint had clearly decided to continue his weird little gifts, yet he'd understood what Charlotte had said to him, he knew what was at stake. Did he not realise that she

could deny ever taking cash from him to sit with Grace and act incredulous if she was ever asked if she'd known about the murder plot? She could get away with her part in this far easier than he could. It wasn't going to be long before someone could ID him for having been at Grace's house, not just on the night he'd abducted her but when Charlotte and Seven had been there to feed the bird.

New information currently filled the local Facebook page and some of the news posts on Charlotte's feed. When an inventory had been done for the contents of Grace's house and she'd looked over it, she'd discovered some of her jewellery was missing. Now the police were after the person who'd stolen it, and speculation was rife that it was the estate agent.

As it was the weekend, Saturday night, Charlotte was glad she wasn't sitting at her desk at work, shitting herself that one of her colleagues was going to see the fear on her face every time she read a new article. And she wouldn't have to sit there worrying until lunchtime when she could nip out to Seven and tell him the latest. He was in bed and hadn't been in the best of moods since she'd taken him out for dinner, but he needed to hear about this because despite him making out this whole charade was absolutely nothing to do with him, he had been in Grace's house with her. He deserved to know what was going on.

She walked to his bedroom down the hallway, and the horrible thought entered her head that the woman in the pawnshop might come forward and say someone had been in to sell the jewellery. It was fine for her, she could make out she didn't know it was stolen, so she'd unlikely get in any trouble, but if Charlotte's description was bandied about then it wasn't going to take long before one of the police officers she'd spoken to twigged it was her.

Yes, she needed to speak to Seven about this; panic was setting in now. Not that she was going to admit to him that she'd taken the jewellery, but maybe just by talking about it she'd feel better.

She tapped on his door, greeted by a grumbled response of, "What do you want?"

He was taking the drug withdrawal really badly. She must have got lucky because after the initial few days of the tormenting taunts from her brain telling her she needed the cocaine, she'd coped relatively well compared to him.

"Um, can I talk to you about something that's on Facebook?" she asked.

"Fucking hell," he shouted.

She wasn't sure whether to retreat or just go in. Fuck it, she went in, recoiling from the smell of unwashed bedding and sweat. She left the door open to air the room out, then went and sat at his desk, waiting for him to get out of bed, but instead he rolled onto his side and faced her, cocooned in the quilt as though he needed it for safety, a shield against whatever she was going to say.

He stared at her.

"Okay," she said, "I know you perhaps don't want to discuss anything to do with the old girl, but I'm afraid we have to. She must have her house up for sale or something because an inventory's been done and some of her jewellery's gone missing."

He shot up to a sitting position, the quilt pooling around his waist. "What?"

"I know."

He eyed her slyly. "Was it you?"

"You what?"

"Was it you? You were upstairs on your own…"

"Who's to say the jewellery was even upstairs? You *were downstairs on* your *own! Fucking hell, you're well rude, you are. I thought we were friends, and yet you're accusing me of nicking from an old lady."*

"Yeah, well, you were going to let someone kill *an old lady…"*

"Fuck off with that, you know damn well it was because I was on drugs, my mind wasn't in the right place, and like I've said to you before, you were just as bad. You seemed to think it was okay for her to be dead just so we could get what we wanted. You conveniently forget about that, don't you."

"So if it wasn't you and it wasn't me…"

"Work it out. It was either Polly or Mint. He was there that night as well, remember. Maybe he came back after we went home."

"I still don't get why he even knocked on the door and then fucked off."

"Maybe only Polly had a key. She could have told him to meet her there, and when no one came to the door, he got in his car again. I don't know, we can speculate all we like, but I don't think he's going to leave us alone, do you? There was the cat and then the syringe and the newspaper clipping. What next?"

"You should never have phoned the police."

"It was the right thing to do."

"You ought to be glad that the others living in that house were so off their faces they didn't even know an old lady was there, otherwise you could have been well in the shit if they'd told someone you went into the attic all the time."

"It wasn't all the time, and I admitted to the police I sat with her anyway."

He was getting on her nerves, always so negative, and so it didn't rub off on her and sour her mood, she stood and brushed imaginary crumbs off her skirt.

"Well, I've kept you up to date, so whatever."

She left the room, shutting the door, going to put on her shoes and coat. She needed to get out of there, especially because a scary thought had come along. What if Grace remembered asking her to go and feed the bird? What if the police then decided to question Charlotte about what else she'd done there? She hadn't told the police that Seven had gone with her, but with the way his conscience was behaving lately, she wouldn't be surprised if he walked into the police station and confessed to having entered the house.

She left the flat and walked to the main front door, taking a deep breath as she always did lately, in case Mint had left something on the doorstep. Thankfully, it was clear, so she trotted down the steps and into the street, heading for a different pub that they'd found. Both of them had agreed they didn't want to drink where Mint might find them again, although she'd argued that considering he'd found out where they lived, then it wasn't a stretch to imagine that he followed them sometimes. That thought spurred her to walk faster. The idea of him lurking in the shadows behind her gave her the bloody creeps.

She turned the corner at the end of the road, and there he was in his car, indicating to turn left into her street. He widened his eyes upon seeing her, clearly surprised to be caught by her address. She took her phone out to message Seven.

CHARLOTTE: QUICKLY GET YOUR ARSE OUT OF BED AND GO AND STAND AT THE LIVING ROOM WINDOW TO SEE IF YOU CAN CATCH MINT UP TO SHIT. HE'S JUST GONE PAST IN HIS CAR AND IS PROBABLY BRINGING US ANOTHER PRESENT. TAKE A PICTURE OF HIM OR VIDEO IT SO WE'VE GOT PROOF HE'S BOTHERING US.

SEVEN: FOR FUCK'S SAKE.

She ignored that and turned to go back down the street, her intention to hide behind a bush and watch what Mint was up to, but his taillights were small pinpricks right at the other end, so he's gone past their flat. He hadn't had any time to jump out and pop something on the doorstep. Now Seven was going to be pissed off because she'd got him out of bed for no reason.

She shrugged and resumed her trek to the pub. It didn't take long to get there, but five minutes was quite a while when your head spun with worry and your gut churned with anxiety. She hated the fact that she was relying on someone else not to open their mouth and get her in trouble—Grace recalling that she'd asked her to feed Pip. But it had been in the newspaper that Polly had been drugging her, and that half the time she would have been in a delirious state so may not have even remembered what she'd discussed with Charlotte. She just had to hope that the evening of the robbery was too hazy for the old lady to recall.

She entered the pub, relieved it was warm inside. She ordered a drink at the bar, a small glass of white wine. She was always conscious of her addictive personality and that one drink could quite easily turn into a whole bottle if she wasn't careful. The fear of becoming reliant on a substance again, like she had with cocaine, frightened her more than she'd ever admit, but that was a good thing, it meant she was still in control and would stop herself from going too far.

She took her drink to sit in a corner out of the way and scrolled her phone for more updates. OLD LADY DISCOVERS MISSING JEWELS *was a misleading headline, making it sound like the jewels had been found, not that they'd been stolen, but the story was a mash-up of the previous ones Charlotte had already read, column inches full of crap, basically clickbait. But the last line had her stomach rolling over.*

> If you saw two people entering 5 Prophet Gardens on the night in question, please contact the police.

So they somehow knew two people had gone in. Charlotte and Seven had entered at the back, so someone had seen them? Had Grace mentioned the keys in the summer house and the police now knew they were for the patio doors, so when they'd gone round asking the neighbours if anyone had seen anything, specifically at the back of the property, it had jogged their memories?

Charlotte's whole body flushed hot, her cheeks prickling from being too warm, so she took her coat off. She sifted through the panic that laughed at her inside her head, the sound of it ricocheting off her brain and threatening to give her a migraine. This couldn't be happening. This couldn't be the way she was caught because of some snoopy fucking neighbours who didn't know the benefits of keeping their nose on their faces instead of in everyone else's business.

She drank some more wine and moved on to the next article. They were all similar, various newspapers writing the same stuff in different words. She kept thinking about their route to Grace's house and how she'd purposely chosen back streets where there were unlikely to be that many cameras.

One thing was certain, unless there was actual footage of Charlotte handing that jewellery over to the pawnbroker, then there was no proof she'd stolen it. Unless there was a camera set up in Grace's bedroom, then who the hell would have seen her put the stuff in her pocket? No one. She had nothing to worry about, this was a secret she'd keep to herself forever, and everything was going to be okay.

She finished her wine and popped her coat back on now that the heat of guilt had dissipated. She left the pub, scanning the area for any sign of Mint hanging around in his car, but she couldn't see him. Hungry, she decided to treat herself to some chips, and she'd get Seven some, too, seeing as he was getting so thin lately. She nipped into the Battered Cod, surprised to find there was no queue, and ordered two portions of chips with salt and vinegar. With the warm packages against her chest, she continued on her way home, eager to get inside and into her pyjamas.

Something smacked into the back of her head from behind, and the chip packets went flying. She registered seeing them floating through the air then crashing onto the pavement, one of them splitting, chips peering out of the jagged hole along with clouds of steam. Then the pain set up in her skull, and the realisation that she'd been walloped seemed to arise way too late. She spun round to get a look at who'd done it, ready to give them a mouthful at the same time as backing down the nearest garden path to knock on a door and ask someone for help, but it was Mint, and for some reason all the fear left her, even though she still ought to be afraid.

"What the fuck was that for?" she whisper-shouted and bent to pick up the unbroken packet of chips.

"I've been at the police station today, being asked questions about some fucking jewellery. Did you tell them I nicked it?"

"No! I didn't even know anything about it until this evening when I read it on my phone, so fuck you, and also fuck you for putting that syringe and whatnot on the doorstep. You're not funny, and you're not scary, so do yourself a favour and just bugger off, okay? Neither of us are interested in getting you in trouble. God, we barely even talk about you, so if you think you're high on our list of conversation topics, you're wrong."

"Just remember to keep my name out of your mouth," he said.

"Like I just told you, we barely talk about you, and it suits me not to talk about you at all. The only reason we do is because you put stuff on the doorstep."

He narrowed his eyes at her. *"It really wasn't you, was it?"*

"No, and it wasn't me the first time either. I did not phone the police at any point, all right?"

"So who told them Grace was in the attic?"

"I don't bloody know, maybe Polly said something to someone. What was your involvement with her anyway? Was it really like she said and you were her boyfriend?"

"No, I wasn't."

"Look…me, you, and Seven don't want to be involved in this, so let's leave it there. This is the last time we'll speak about it. You can trust me, I didn't even tell them that you'd paid me to sit with her, or have you conveniently forgotten that?"

"Shit just keeps going around in my head, and I get paranoid, that's all."

"Don't. Stick to your story. You rented a room to Polly, and what happened in it, you have no idea."

He nodded and gestured to the chips on the floor. *"Sorry about that."*

"Doesn't matter, I'll share these ones with Seven; they always give big portions anyway. He doesn't need

to know he had a packet of his own and you fucked it up."

"I'd, err, I'd best be going then. Remember, mouth shut."

"Aww, piss off, will you? Enough now."

She walked away, her legs shaking, her head throbbing. She made it home without any more assaults, which was always a bonus, and the chips were still warm enough when she took them out of the packet. She shared them between two plates and took them into the living room where Seven sat on sofa with a monk on.

"He didn't leave anything," he said.

"No, because he decided to do something else instead." Charlotte handed him his plate of chips.

"Cheers. What was that then?"

"He waited for me to leave the chippy and then smacked me in the back of the head."

"Fucking hell… This is all getting a bit much now."

"I thought the same, but we came to an agreement that all three of us are going to keep our mouths shut about each other. I think I've convinced him I didn't phone the police, so unless you open your gob and tell him, then he'll never know."

"I'm not going to be saying anything."

"Good."

They ate their chips in silence, the muted telly throwing out flickers of light from some police drama playing out on the screen. Just the sight of a copper in uniform scared her now.

"I want to disappear and never be found," Seven said.

"Yeah, well, I don't think it's that easy, but I know what you mean."

"We could do it. Change our names. Move to another Estate or out of London completely."

She rolled her eyes. "That's going to cost money, and I can't earn extra by sitting with an old lady, and there's no way I'm asking my parents again."

"I'll think of something. I can't stand being here anymore. I've got to get out, get a fresh start. Grow my hair and a beard or something."

It wasn't like she hadn't thought of this herself, and it was something she could mull over in the coming days while she kept an eye on the newsfeed. She was tempted to go and see the pawnbroker but thought better of it. The woman might not take any notice of what was going on in a place ten miles away. She might not even be aware that the jewellery had been stolen. And she hadn't cared if it was anyway.

Charlotte convinced herself she was safe for now and got up to take the plates to the kitchen and get a couple of paracetamol for her aching head.

Chapter Eighteen

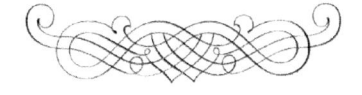

Mint hadn't expected to be here, but it was a bloody good stroke of fortune that he was. He'd just been about to enter Timmons' street when he'd caught sight of the front door opening of the house belonging to the Irishman and the pregnant woman. Light had spilled out onto the path in their garden, and he'd pressed himself against a high wall on the corner so he couldn't be seen.

The man had kissed the woman. "I'll be back in a few hours."

"Okay. I thought you going in at night wasn't supposed to be happening anymore."

"Same here."

He'd kissed her again, got in a car, and driven away. She'd closed the door, and Mint had listened to the tinkle as she'd put a chain in place. He'd pushed himself off the wall and went to cross the road when headlights in the other direction swerved into the street. He'd darted into someone else's garden and hid behind a bush, watching through gaps in the leaves.

Those fucking twins had parked outside Timmons' house, getting out with a dog and going to knock on the door. They'd asked where Mint was, and Timmons let them in. At the time Mint had been furious, but then the scrape of a chain being pulled across had reached him, and the woman had come out. She'd held a black bag and paused to look at the twins' van. Her frown was clear as day in the light of the streetlamp, then she went down the side of her house, probably to pop the rubbish in the wheelie bin.

Mint had crept out from his hiding place and legged it into her house, and now, here she was, crying at her kitchen island, her eyes red-rimmed, her rosy-tipped nose running.

"What do you want?" she whispered. "If it's about the bins, we're going to be leaving them at the kerb from now on. We didn't know it was an actual thing, we thought your dad was imposing his own rules."

"I couldn't give a shit about the fucking bins, just be quiet while I figure out what I'm going to do."

"Why are you here?"

He thought about how he'd hidden behind the kitchen door, and when she'd come back he'd jumped out and slapped a hand over her mouth so she didn't scream. The last thing he wanted was the twins hearing her.

"There are people around my dad's that I don't want to see."

"The Brothers."

"Yeah."

"Are you hiding from them? Have you done something wrong?"

"They don't want me selling on their Estate, that's all. They even sent someone to stab me. Now who *does* that?"

"I'm sorry that happened to you, but can you please leave because you're scaring me."

"I'm not leaving until they've gone, and like I've already told you, if you scream I'll stab you in the stomach. Your baby will die, and it'll be all your fault."

She looked at him as though he were a monster, and he supposed he was, saying shit like that, but if there was one thing he knew, a pregnant woman would do anything to save her child—or she would if she was decent, and he reckoned she was more than that. She was a posh type, had probably been used to having money all her life. Her pyjamas were a hell of a lot better quality than Charlotte's. He couldn't believe he'd gone there to shag her, and thanked his lucky stars that she she'd woken up, really, otherwise he might have gone through with it out of desperation.

He had a better-looking woman right here in front of him, but her big stomach turned him off, although he supposed he could fuck her from behind. It was that fireplace and mantel thing all over again, and it was doing his head in.

"I won't scream," she said calmly. "I don't think you actually want to hurt me anyway."

Air puffed out between his lips. "Are you doing that thing, making me think you understand me? I can't see you being able to do that, love, because I don't even understand myself. I don't even know why I'm in here."

"You said it was to hide."

"Well, yeah, it is, but I should have just fucked off somewhere else until the twins had gone, but instead I came in here and scared you. I've done shit in my life that I'm not proud of, it's like I act now and think later."

"We all make decisions we regret."

"Believe me, I bet I've made worse decisions than you."

"Depends whether you think getting your husband killed is a bad decision."

His eyebrows rose. "Pardon me? You want the Irishman dead?"

"No, it was someone else I was married to."

"Fucking hell. Why are you telling me this?"

"So you know that everyone has a secret. You're not special."

Oddly, what she'd said made him feel better. If she was telling the truth, that meant even posh totty had problems in their lives, they could be failures, too.

"So what happened with your other man?" he asked.

"He was going abroad a lot for work, but what I didn't know was that he had another woman over there. He was also bringing drugs into the country. I had been so completely hoodwinked that I'm afraid I let my anger get the better of me and asked for help. He's no longer with us."

Bloody hell, he was kind of glad he'd only had to contend with Ashley taking the house. She could have acted so much worse towards him. She hadn't even divorced him while he'd been in prison—he supposed that would soon be on the way. Maybe, now that he'd just heard this little tale of a woman scorned, he ought to let Ashley know Timmons' address so she could get the ball rolling if she wanted to. She didn't need to chase him for child support because that was still paid without fail out of the tenants' rent money.

"I asked The Brothers for help," she said casually, getting up to lay her hands on her lower back and push her stomach out in a stretch. "They were ever so good, so if you need somebody in your corner, I suggest going to them."

"I can't, not now they've had me stabbed. Fucking hell, why didn't I listen to the warnings? Why did I keep selling? Why do I always think I know best?"

"No idea. Would you like a coffee?"

He nodded, watching her go to a fancy machine on the side, the type in coffee shops. "When's the baby due?"

"September, although it still feels forever away. I'm going to have to go to the toilet soon, just so you know. Feel free to come with me if you have to."

"It's fine, I'll wait outside the door."

He'd already seen she didn't have her phone. Maybe she'd left it upstairs when she'd come to the door to see the Irishman off. She carried a coffee over to him, taking a can out of the fridge for herself, a ginger beer. He remembered Ashley having heartburn and swearing by ginger biscuits.

"The toilet?" he asked.

"I'm actually a bit hot. Do you mind if I open the patio door?"

He did mind—a spike of worry poked into his stomach. "Remember what I said, about stabbing the baby."

She nodded and reached for a key on the worktop, inserting it and then pulling the door across to let in some air. She stepped out slowly, lifting her face to the dark sky and sifting her hands through her long hair as if she needed to get it off her neck. He eyed her warily.

"We've had nice weather lately," she said.

"Been a bit too hot for me to be honest. Fucking heatwaves do my nut in."

"Same. Do you have kids?"

"Two, but they don't even know me. They were young when I went to prison, and I was going to go and see them when I got out, but Ashley, that's their mum, she's not interested in anything like that. Can't say I blame her. And she's got a new bloke."

"That's a shame. Maybe they'll come to you when they're older and they can make their own mind up."

"Yeah." He reached over for his coffee.

Something slammed, and he whipped round to see she'd closed the door and was putting the key in the lock and twisting it, looking through the glass at him, her stare defiant. Then she screamed, and kept screaming and screaming.

Mint panicked and put the coffee down. He couldn't get out the back, so his only escape was the front, and he'd insisted she put the chain on and double-locked the door after he'd taken his hand off her mouth and warned her what would happen if she fucked him around. His plan to give him time to escape out the back should the Irishman come home had gone tits up, and now he fumbled with the chain, and once he finally got that sorted, his hand shook as he tried to push the snib up on the Yale. At last, he yanked the door open and shot out onto the path, glancing to the left over a low brick wall at George, Greg, and Timmons standing in his father's garden.

He had no time to hang about. He pelted up the pavement, running as fast as he was able to with a stitched-up stab wound. Out of breath by the time he reached the corner, he legged it to the sound of shouts behind him and the bark of that fucking dog. At the next corner, he dared to peer over his shoulder. No one followed. He slowed to a walk, his chest tight, sweat breaking out at his temples. He'd ring for a taxi in a minute, get the driver to take him to Ashley, plead with her to let him stay in the spare room until he could get his affairs in order.

He stepped out to cross the road, fishing around in his coat pocket to get his phone, but it got caught up in a glove. He tugged, then came the sound of an engine far too late. He turned to his left, shock rendering him stock-still as he stared at a van hurtling towards him. It smacked into the side of his leg, shooting him into the air, the pain instant. He landed on the bonnet, grasping at the windscreen wipers for something to hold on to, staring through at George who glared at him. Then the van stopped abruptly, the momentum flinging Mint onto the tarmac. When the engine revved again and one of the wheels rode over his ankles, he wished he was dead.

Chapter Nineteen

George bundled Mint into the back of the van with a whining Ralph who flopped his front paws over the man's body as if that would help to stop him from getting up. George shut the door. A couple of people had come out of their houses to see what was going on, but Greg had handed them hush-money envelopes and sent them on their way, his threats still lingering in the air.

George got in the passenger side, sticking on his seat belt. "Bet that fucking hurt."

"That was the whole point of me knocking him over." Greg set off, calling into the back, "If you don't shut up whimpering, I'm going to have to stop this van, and my brother will get in the back with you and *make* you shut up."

"My fucking ankles are broken!"

George smirked. "Be a dear and don't gripe about it."

Greg laughed to himself. "You're a hard-hearted bastard."

"Yeah, well, he doesn't deserve any sympathy after what he's done."

"I just sold drugs, for fuck's sake!" Mint shouted. "Do you really think it's okay to stab someone in town and then run them over, all because of a few baggies?"

"But it's more than baggies, isn't it," George said, his temper rising at the fact this pleb really didn't understand what he'd done wrong. Was he that entitled he thought he had the right to sell wherever he wanted? "You can't tell me you haven't grown up knowing about leaders and their rules. You knew exactly what you were doing."

"I didn't want to pay protection money, all right? I didn't have to on the last Estate I lived on."

"Because Greaves didn't know you were selling, that's why."

"How do you know?"

"Leaders talk."

"Shit."

"Yeah, shit, so pack it in with the bollocks, because we know damn well what kind of man you are. If you want something then you're going to take it, isn't that right?"

"What are you on about?" Mint panted. His legs must really be hurting.

"That's why you went to see Sharon, wasn't it."

"Who the fuck's Sharon, the woman next door to Timmons?"

"You'd know Sharon as Charlotte."

"*What?*"

"She had to change her name because of you. She felt she had no choice but to leave the Greaves Estate, even though you'd been arrested and put on remand. She cut ties with her family so they'd be safe from anything you might send their way. As in, she was worried you had the kind of contacts who'd hurt her parents if it was clear they knew something."

"Knew what?"

"I don't know, we didn't get that deep into it, but suffice to say she was convinced she needed to disappear."

"I thought she dobbed me in to the police, but even so, I never touched her family. I didn't even get anyone to find out where she was."

"No, you just waited until you got out so you could do it yourself."

"I didn't. When I saw her on the day I got stabbed, I didn't expect it."

"So we're supposed to believe it was just a coincidence that you were outside the café she manages."

"She manages it?"

"Yeah, for us."

"It *was* a coincidence, though, I swear to God."

"Yet you went in the Shiny Fork and asked her questions."

"I needed to know if it was her or not."

"And what did she say?"

"That she didn't do anything. I believed her."

"So why did you wait for her near the taxi rank?"

"I just wanted to talk."

"She went to the pub with you, you got your talk, but then you broke into her flat. What the fuck are you playing at, sunshine? And. Stop. Fucking. Panting."

"I can't help it!"

"I'm going to enjoy killing you."

"Oh God, no…"

"What did you think we were doing, taking you home to Daddy?"

"Please, I'll move off the Estate. You'll never see me again."

"Now why don't I believe you? That's right, because when you had several warnings to stop selling drugs, you carried on regardless."

"I mean it this time, I'll do as I'm told."

"People always say that when they know they're at the end of the line. I hear you've got a wife and kids. I assume the missus will get your houses in seven years when you're pronounced dead not just missing."

"They're in both of our names. I was supposed to get them changed to just mine after I came out. I didn't get around to it."

"The bloke who collects the rents. What happens there?"

"He's a mate from years ago. He keeps an eye on it all. The rents go into a bank account."

"I see. Is it a bank account with just your name on it?"

"Yeah."

"Then we'll get that changed. Your tenants will be informed they need to set up a direct debit into a different account. One belonging to your wife. We wouldn't want her waiting all those years for the accumulated cash. We'll get Greaves to pop and see her, let her know the score and that she isn't to report you missing for at least two years. That way the money being rerouted from the tenants won't look suspicious. Your debit and credit cards will still be used periodically—you'll be a good boy and give us the PINs. I assume you've had your post redirected to Mr Timmons' house."

"Yes… yes…"

"I'd say it's working out jolly nicely then, wouldn't you? Ashley will be informed that she owns your business now—the legitimate one as a landlord. We'll send someone round to Mr

Timmons' house to relieve him of any drugs you've got hidden there."

"Leave him alone."

"I don't think you're in a position to tell me what to do," George said. "We can have a chat with him ourselves to see whether he was aware the drugs were there—if they even are. You might have been a nice son and decided not to get him involved, but I doubt it. Just by storing stuff at his place makes him involved, we'll just have to decide whether or not he should be punished for it."

"Fucking hell, he's just an old man. He hasn't done jack shit."

"So you say, but you've got an awful habit of lying, so excuse me if I don't take your word as gospel. We're here now."

George got out of the van which Greg had parked with the rear facing the front of the building. George opened the warehouse, turning to find Greg waiting for him. Greg leaned in the van and stuffed a rag into Mint's mouth, then they both got inside, Ralph jumping out to disappear into the warehouse. Greg gripped the bloke under the armpits, and George took great pleasure in clamping his meaty hands around the broken ankles. Mint screamed, although it was muffled by the cloth. They quickly took him inside and down to the cellar. Greg remained with him while George nipped up to lock the van and the front door.

Ralph got the zoomies and hared around the warehouse then shot down into the cellar. George went to the sideboard by the table, took out a couple of dog bowls and a pouch of food. He went downstairs, filling one bowl with water from the hose on the wall, emptying the pouch into the other. With the collie happily munching away, George helped Greg finish stripping Mint. They attached manacles around his wrists, and Greg went over to the crank to turn it. The chains rose, taking Mint up with them. He hung above the trapdoor and tried to find purchase with his toes, screeching at the pain the movement had caused, but they hovered too high. He sagged, clearly defeated.

George walked around him, glancing at his meat and two veg, laughing at the size of them. There was nothing wrong with them, he just wanted the man to feel humiliated, like Sharon had when she'd realised what he'd had in mind when he'd hovered his lips near hers earlier. Fucking bastard.

George did a roundhouse kick, planting the sole of his boot on Mint's cock. The man's lips spread where he opened his mouth to scream, and George pulled the cloth away so he could listen to the agony in the screech. He dropped it to the floor on top of Mint's clothes, sweeping them away with the side of his foot. Greg got on with lighting the wood-burning stove to dispose of the fabric.

"Please," Mint gasped out, "I promise I'll never do a bad thing again."

"I don't believe you. People like you have a habit of making these promises, but then they break them. Did you know that Charlotte has tried to be a good person ever since that shit happened with Grace? Life's kicked her in the teeth since she moved to Cardigan, and she swears blind it's karma out to get her, so she keeps trying to be nice in the hope that karma's nice to her. Recently she helped this bloke from Jamaica who was trapped in a gang. She could have walked away from him—I mean, the shit he was involved in was pretty fucking bad—but she didn't, she stuck her neck out. She's felt guilty for so many things, a lot of them to do with when she took drugs; they changed her, turned her a bit selfish for a while, but that's what happens when people get addicted. And you're coining it in, not giving two shits that you're affecting someone to the point that they agree to sit with an old lady who might actually be killed. Think of all the other people you've affected."

"I don't force anyone to buy drugs."

"No, if they know there's a steady supply from you, they're going to keep coming back, aren't they. Did Ashley actually know what you did on the side?"

"No, she wouldn't have stood for it."

"Good for her. Right, I suppose we ought to get started then."

"Oh God, what are you going to do?"

"Hang tight and you'll find out, won't you."

Chapter Twenty

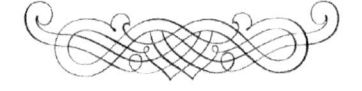

Sometimes fate sent you down weird paths, ones you really, really shouldn't go down, ones she should ignore, but once Charlotte saw Grace getting on a bus with the aid of her walking stick, she'd made the decision to get on after her. She paid the fare and then scanned the seats, walking towards Grace who

recognised her the second she sat in the adjacent seat, her eyes lighting up.

"Oh, it's you!"

It was a surreal experience for Charlotte, knowing she'd been part of a murder plot and the victim was treating her as though she were a friend. Guilt swamped her, yet at the same time she was going to take the opportunity to continue chatting to Grace for the duration of the journey.

"Oh, how lovely to see you again." Charlotte smiled at her, hoping she sounded sincere. "I'm really glad I've seen you, because I've been worrying about you ever since everything came out. I had no idea that you were being kept there like that…"

"I know, the police told me that I thought you were a carer and you'd only sat with me because you felt sorry for me. I don't remember an awful lot of being in that room to be honest, and I'm glad, because it sounds like it was dreadful. And as for Polly…"

"Would you like to go somewhere for a cup of coffee? I mean, if you're going to town, that is."

"Yes, that would be lovely."

They didn't speak again until they sat in a café at the bus station. Charlotte had paid for a pot of tea each and a slice of Victoria sponge, the least she could do, considering.

"I'm so glad you recognised me," Charlotte lied.

"Of course I do, because you were kind to me. I recall you sitting with me but don't know what times of the day. Everything seemed to be one time in there. I can't explain it, but there wasn't night or day or anything like that. I don't even remember eating, but apparently Polly fed me."

"I read in the paper that she was your husband's carer."

"And isn't it awful that someone we both trusted turned out to be so awful, and all over money?"

"Terrible."

"I'm surprised she admitted it, although she blamed it on that landlord of yours."

"I doubt very much he had anything to do with it."

"He was the estate agent who was going to sell my house."

Charlotte swallowed. "So was he really *an estate agent?"*

"Oh yes, the police looked into him, and everything was above board. As far as I'm aware they think he genuinely wanted to help me sell the house. He claims to not know who Polly is, whereas she's claiming they were boyfriend and girlfriend and he was in on everything. It's all a bit of a haze to me because I don't

understand where they were supposed to have met, as he's saying he never met her at all."

Surely the police would be able to work it out that he was lying, but maybe Polly had come across as unhinged and Mint had truly got away with it by the skin of his teeth.

"He's a property owner as well, you know," Grace said. "He doesn't just own the house that we lived in but also two more, as well as a family home."

Charlotte's stomach rolled over, something it seemed to do a lot of these days. "Um, which estate agent does he work at?"

"I didn't know this until the police told me because the card he gave me only had a phone number on it, but he's with Anderson and Peters round the corner from here."

The same estate agent Charlotte had visited to get the new flat. Had he seen her details at some point and that was how he knew where to come to leave the cat? And what kind of man was he to be an estate agent and *a drug dealer? How did that even happen?*

"He always seemed nice enough to me when he collected my rent," Charlotte said, "and I'd be more inclined to think that it was Polly who cooked this up all by herself. It said in the paper that she rented the

attic room, there's a tenancy agreement and everything."

"Is there really? I haven't heard about that, but then I don't necessarily want a blow-by-blow account of what's going on in the investigation because…because there are memories I don't want to remember."

"You should have said if you find this difficult. We could have talked about something else."

"I don't mind talking about it on my terms." Grace picked up her cup, her hands surprisingly steady for a woman of her age. She sipped, staring out of the window. "I should have known Polly would turn funny. She kept mentioning how Frank had left her that money and probing to see whether I was going to do the same. She came to visit me after he died, and I honestly thought it was because she cared about me being on my own, but all along it was so I left all of my money to her. Dreadful woman. In that attic, I thought I was in a hospice because of her nurse uniform…"

Seeing the pain in Grace's eyes had Charlotte feeling bad again. How wrong of her to have been so hooked on drugs that she'd agreed to anything in order to make enough money to get herself clean. Murder was a big thing, yet she'd convinced herself that sitting with Grace was perfectly fine while the clock tick-tocked towards her imminent death.

But Charlotte had to make herself feel better by knowing she'd stopped it in the end. She'd done the right thing when it mattered. If she didn't acknowledge that, then she risked spiralling into a pit of depression, like Seven. She swore he'd grabbed on to wallowing in the doldrums so he had something to take his mind off the drugs. He'd switched his addiction for something just as damaging, only it wasn't his body that would be harmed, it was his mental health.

"I hope you can try and put this behind you," Charlotte said. "I know it'll never go away, but maybe it'll fade so it's not as painful."

Grace smiled. "It's already fading, love. I feel so much safer now I don't live alone. I only have to press a button and someone will come and help me." She cut off a piece of her cake and held the fork partway to her mouth. "I'm going to need to sell the house anyway to help me pay for the new place, but for the moment I have money in the bank I'd saved for years with Frank, so I'm not going to become destitute or starve."

"Good."

Charlotte changed the subject to the weather — boring but necessary so she didn't dwell on what had happened. It was all very well seeing that Grace was fine on the outside, so what on earth had happened on the inside? Was she anxious? Did she have nightmares about being in the attic? Had irreparable damage been done? Of course it bloody had. She might even suffer from PTSD.

Tears stung Charlotte's eyes. God, she wished she'd never set eyes on Mint. But then was it fair to blame him when she'd been the one to approach him for drugs, she'd been the one to take up his offer of moving into the house, and she'd been the one who was greedy enough to hold out her palm for the cash he'd placed on it after she'd sat with Grace. Yes, Mint had a hand in this, but Charlotte had made her own decisions. She had to own them and move on.

She was pissing herself off keep going over and over it in her head.

She was dying to ask Grace about the jewellery, but she'd look a right cow if she did that, seeing as the woman had said she preferred to talk about everything on her own terms. Still, the need was there and it wasn't about to go away, so she racked her brain to think of a way to bring the subject up where it wouldn't be obvious she was probing for information. She spied Grace's wedding ring.

"That's got some lovely patterns on it." Charlotte gestured to the white-gold band with swirls engraved on it. Some of them were smoother where she must

have worn the ring for years and it had rubbed against things over time.

Grace stared down at it, a small smile playing about her lips that were surrounded by a concertina of wrinkles. "It's the only ring I have left. My engagement ring was stolen along with my other jewellery."

"I read about that in the news. I'm so sorry. Some people are bloody awful, aren't they, the way they think nothing of taking what doesn't belong to them."

"I can only think it was Polly or the man who took me from my house."

Charlotte frowned. Something wasn't adding up here. Grace had said that Mint wasn't anything to do with this, that he was just an estate agent, yet she'd just mentioned the man who'd taken her from her house. On one of the evenings Charlotte had sat with her, Grace had said about having the estate agent round for dinner. Had she forgotten she'd told her that? Did she know damn well Mint was involved but she was keeping her mouth shut? Had he somehow got hold of her since the police had been made aware, threatening her to keep quiet?

"That would have been my landlord," Charlotte said, "but you've not long told me it couldn't have

been him. He was due round for dinner, do you remember telling me that?"

Grace shook her head. "I told you no such thing. No one was coming round for dinner."

Something was definitely up. The old woman had been spooked, Charlotte was convinced of it, and maybe Grace had put two and two together regarding the jewellery and Charlotte's visit to feed Pip, but she was pretending that *hadn't happened, too.*

"So you think it could be the man who took you from your house who stole your jewellery? Who was that then if it wasn't my landlord?"

"I have no idea."

"It said in the papers that Polly was blaming Mint…"

"No, no, she's got it all wrong. I don't want to talk about this anymore, it's all so distressing. My jewellery is gone, and I've accepted that. It's time to move on now. I don't have that much longer left, and I want to enjoy the rest of my life, not sit there worrying about being kidnapped and my poor budgie dying." Grace wiped a tear away with her fingertip and got on with eating her cake.

"What have you been watching on the telly lately, then?" Charlotte asked, making it clear she'd understood the memo.

Grace smiled and launched into a conversation about EastEnders, *and all Charlotte could think was that the crap that had happened wouldn't sound believable if it appeared on that programme.*

Life was indeed stranger than fiction.

Chapter Twenty-One

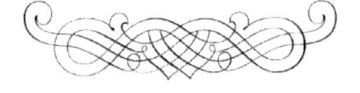

For some reason, no sooner had Mint been strung up than George had ordered for him to be lowered. Because of his broken ankles, Mint sat on the floor. What were they going to do to him? When he'd been hanging he'd anticipated a beating, had prepared himself for it, almost, but this change had him uneasy.

He had no idea where the fuck he was. He'd had to close his eyes from the pain when he'd been carried in. It was a cellar, he knew that much, but was it in some big fuck-off house or elsewhere? He imagined it being in an abandoned building, hidden behind vines and forgotten memories, the place once vibrant but now dilapidated, somewhere no one would think he'd be taken. That's what he do, choose somewhere remote.

Mildew, the smell of it was getting right up his nose. The space was only lit in one corner by a free-standing lamp. It created eerie shadows in the corners. There was a creepy feel to it, the stone walls like something out of the olden days. The air was thick with not only tension but the humidity of the day—a good rainstorm was needed.

It seemed like even the walls held their breath while he waited for one of the twins to speak. He spotted a monitor on the wall at the bottom of the stairs showing a view of what he assumed was outside: a large space for parking vehicles and a road, nothing like the sweeping drive he'd conjured in his mind. He didn't have much knowledge about the twins and who they were—

if he did, then maybe he'd know damn well where he was.

George grinned at him. "I was going to beat the crap out of you while you hung there, defenceless, but I fancy a bit of fun. Let's see what you've got. Let's see you fight back." He looked at his brother. "Help him stand up, will you?"

Greg emerged from a dark corner by a table. "Just don't hit me by mistake, bruv."

George had changed into a forensic suit and slapped a fist against his gloved palm, the thuds of the smacks matching Mint's heartbeat, then the twin shadow-boxed, warming up, determination in his expression.

Mint was going to have to improvise. He'd never fought like this before, had only ever given someone a clip round the earhole, so this new experience was likely to go wrong considering he faced a man like George. Greg slipped his arms under Mint's armpits and brought him to standing, the pain excruciating and shooting up Mint's legs. Just the agony alone was going to tire him out, so if George expected him to fight then he'd better think again. Greg was holding him up easily, but how long could he do that for? The bloke was beefy, but surely he had a limit.

George charged forward, fists up. Mint would have dodged out of the way if he could, but instead he swung a right hook. It didn't make contact. George's fist ploughed into Mint's stomach.

"Fucking weak piece of shit," George said.

Mint raised his arm, ready to strike, but George sidestepped then spun round so they stood face to face again. He landed a vicious uppercut to Mint's chin. Mint's head snapped back, but it didn't bash into Greg's face as he'd expected. Had they played this game with someone before? Had Greg acted as the puppet master while George tortured someone?

"Come on, my old son, hit me."

Mint swallowed down the pain from his legs and raised his fist. He walloped George in the cheekbone, but the man didn't even stagger. They exchanged blows one after the other. Mint's eye swelled, fluid collecting under the skin and pushing to break free. The pressure there was intense. He attempted several more hits, and with each missed punch, his embarrassment burned brighter. Going by the look on George's face, the bloke wanted him to try harder—maybe he got off on someone inflicting pain on him—so Mint doubled his efforts. He drew on his reserve energy, lifting his left hand as though to punch George in the temple, but changing his mind at the last minute, smacking him with the right fist instead.

George took a step back, smiled, then lurched forward and pummelled Mint in the stomach, hit after spiteful hit, the sound of fists against flesh echoing. Mint tried to duck and dive, to thump him back, but honestly, what was the point? This was only for George's enjoyment, for him to gloat that he was the better fighter, yet Mint was at a severe disadvantage, the odds against him even if his ankles *weren't* broken. Exhaustion hit him in a wave, and he allowed all of his muscles to relax. Greg still held him tight.

George's eyes widened, and it was clear he was going to take this opportunity to fight unobstructed. A cowardly thing to do, but Mint failed to care anymore. He was going to die, no matter what he did or said, so to plead for his life or fight back was pointless. He wouldn't give George the satisfaction.

George delivered a hard left jab, dancing on his toes, shadow-boxing again, then he swung his body round in a complete circle, raising his leg to kick Mint in the bollocks. All the air left Mint's lungs, bursting out in an *oof*, his eyes watering. He blinked the tears away and stared at his opponent whose eyes glinted with some kind of madness. Whatever fuelled the nutter propelled him forward, and a savage flurry of punches hit Mint's face. His nose popped, pain spreading across his cheekbones, another sheen of tears filling his eyes and spilling down.

Greg let Mint go. On his knees, Mint flopped forward, not even bothering to put his hands out to brace himself. He crashed onto the floor, his legs on the trapdoor, his cheek on a cold flagstone that mercifully eased some of the pain in his face—frozen peas would've been better, but he didn't have the luxury of those. George stood over him; Mint sensed him rather than saw him, and he just couldn't summon the energy to give a fuck.

He let his eyes close, the swollen one so sore, and his mind drifted. He'd bet this cellar held many secrets, the ones regarding him shiny and new, stored inside the walls that had watched him take a beating. George's laughter echoed, merging with the bouts of laughter in Mint's head, of Ashley and the kids giggling, the times when he'd made them happy, when he'd actually been there to do so. God, he'd been such a bastard.

The peace down here shouldn't be so welcome, but he embraced it, floating off into a darkness that weirdly didn't scare him like he'd thought it would. He allowed it shunt him along to wherever he had to go, thinking that death was blacker than any black he'd ever seen, but it was soft and calming, the kind of darkness you could sink into.

Dying wasn't so bad after all.

Chapter Twenty-Two

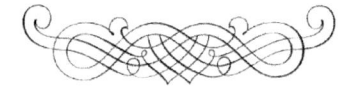

The lamp in the corner flickered, ghosts made out of shadows dancing on the walls—eerie as fuck, considering Mint looked like he was dying. Which didn't make sense, because George hadn't hit him *that* hard, unless he'd given one of those punches that did something lethal to the brain, turning a simple fight into a fatal one.

The man on the floor was a sorry piece of shit when George thought about it, making a flurry of bad decisions that had brought him to this cellar, his breathing getting shallower by the second. George wanted him to look up at him, for his face to be the last one Mint saw, but the bloke likely didn't have enough energy. He'd only be able to see him out of one eye anyway; the other had rapidly swollen, a purple egg sitting on his cheekbone.

Further lending a creepy air to the proceedings was Greg who stood in the darkest corner, a tall and wide shadow man.

"I don't think you've got much time, bruv. He's on his last legs." Greg stepped back into the light, selecting a knife from the tool table. "Are you doing it or am I?"

"Let me try and get something out of him first. A sorry at least." George crouched, roughly pushing up Mint's top eyelids and holding them open. "Are you going to say sorry? It doesn't have to be to anyone specific, but showing a bit of remorse wouldn't go amiss."

"I didn't mean to…" Mint gasped for air, his bad eye rolling.

"Didn't mean to what? Try and kill an old lady? Yeah, we've read the articles about you. You upset a lot of people, but then I expect you know that. You touched a lot of lives, and not in a good way."

"Please, I just..."

"You just what? Crashed through your life doing whatever the fuck you wanted? Actually, even if you said sorry it wouldn't be enough."

"I'll stop selling drugs. I'll move off your Estate."

"It's too late."

Mint's sore eye stared at George but darted from side to side every now and again as though it was looking for a way out for him because he couldn't do it himself, searching for a glimmer of hope when it was obvious there wasn't any. The human spirit was a dickhead like that, didn't quite get the gist of the matter until the last knockings.

George grabbed hold of Mint's chin with his other hand, bending closer. He gripped tighter, wishing he could break his jaw by squeeze alone. "Have you felt any regret yet?"

Mint tried to nod. It seemed he'd finally grasped how futile it was to fight, to even want to live, as his eye rolled back, showing only the white. George hoped the weight of the man's actions we're suffocating him now, swirling around in his mind until he couldn't stand it any longer. He let the eyelids go. Let his face go. He stood and took the knife from Greg, then knelt behind Mint. There was no point in delaying the inevitable. George gripped Mint's hair and pulled his head back, exposing his throat. A quick slice across it with the blade, then Mint's last breath sucked in and puffed out, dissipating into the muggy air.

And the wanker didn't even mention his poor old mum.

Chapter Twenty-Three

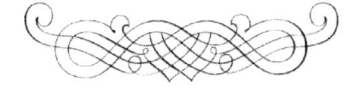

Charlotte and Seven were en route to the chippy, the only way she could get her flatmate out in the evenings so he didn't wallow in his bed from the second he walked in from work. It was a dark Friday , so they had the weekend ahead of them. She'd got Seven to promise that he'd go food shopping with her tomorrow. It wasn't enough that he was leaving the house for

work. He stayed in the flat at all other times unless she bullied him to go out with her. It was as if he felt safe within their shared accommodation, yet she felt the opposite because she was always on edge that Mint would go against his word of leaving them alone and put another present on the steps.

She hadn't seen Grace again since their visit to the café, convincing herself that the old woman had meant it when she'd said she wanted to move on, that the jewellery was gone and that was the end of it. Charlotte had allowed herself to believe she was free and clear, at least from the old woman's perspective, but that didn't mean the police weren't still snooping into the theft behind the scenes.

Social media had gone quiet regarding Grace's story, and it had given Charlotte a sense of security for the past week or two. She'd persuaded herself that none of it had happened, especially when she was at work with her mind occupied. Then when Seven came out of his room, which wasn't often, she was reminded of how she'd met him at the house and everything that had followed.

"What are you going to have to eat tonight?" she asked, looping her arm around his.

"I might have a sausage as well as chips."

"Steady," she joked, her way of letting him know she'd noticed him only eating a few chips from her packet. *"You've got really thin, so I'm glad you've decided to eat a bit more."*

He didn't answer, and she was about to launch into some bullshit that had happened at work earlier on when a big bloke stepped out from behind the bushes, blocking their path. She opened her mouth to scream out her shock but then saw it was that fucking prick, Mint.

"What do you want now?" she asked.

"We need to talk, but not where we can be seen."

"It didn't bother you being seen when you whacked me over the head."

"No arguing. I mean it, this is serious."

"We're not going anywhere with you until you give me an inkling of what this is about. And I don't mean what happened in general, I'm on about specifics."

Mint leaned to the side to look behind Seven. "I heard you had a chinwag with Grace."

"Oh, that."

"Yeah, that. Go and wait behind the shops, we'll talk there."

He spun round and stalked off. Charlotte gawped at the space he'd occupied and then stared at Seven who looked like he was about to cry. She placed a hand on his shoulder, and that was it, the floodgates opened. He sank into a squat, his forearms resting on his thighs, his head bowed, shoulders shaking with his sobs. Fucking hell, this was all she needed, dealing with a mental breakdown.

She told herself off for being so mean. She was supposed to be turning over a new leaf and becoming a better person, and what better way to do it than get her mate back on his feet. She did that and let him hug her, gripping him back just as tightly because, shit, they'd been through some crap together, and while it was supposed to have ended with them moving out of Mint's place, it kept dragging on. She allowed herself to have a proper cry with him, guiding him to someone's garden wall and urging him to sit. Mint would have to wait.

"Fucking hell." Seven sniffed. "I can't keep doing this. I'm a bag of nerves every time I see that bloke. Why won't he just fuck off?"

"Because he likes to have control. You know what he was like when he was dealing drugs to us. He got off on how desperate we were."

"What do you reckon he wants?"

"God knows. Maybe Grace told him I'd questioned his involvement to do with the jewellery. For all we *know he could be paying her regular visits, threatening her and stuff."*

"Yeah, I reckon you're right. We're not going to be able to get away from him, you know. Not unless we have new identities and disappear."

"I've looked into that. There's deed poll. That costs fifty quid, and at least that way we can still get benefits and jobs and whatever because our National Insurance numbers will stay the same—I think so anyway. We want to be able to hide ourselves, but there's something that's going to be a bit of a problem. Apparently, your name change is advertised in The Gazette.*"*

"What Gazette?*"*

"I don't know, that's just what it said on Google, but I can't imagine Mint looking at name changes in there anyway, can you?"

"No, but what if there's some online place where he can make a search and it brings our changes up?"

She wasn't going to say out loud what she'd been thinking of for quite some time, that if Mint no longer existed then they wouldn't have a problem. Or maybe she should *talk to Seven about it. Considering he didn't have a conscience regarding Grace being killed, maybe he wouldn't have one with Mint either.*

"We should kill him," she said.
"What?"

She turned to him. He stared at her with his mouth open.

"Make it look like an accident," she went on. "A quick push in the Thames after he's been knocked on the head."

"You're serious."

"Yep."

"We're going to have to save again, two flat deposits this time."

She nodded. "Okay. We'll go and see him now around the back of the shops and arrange to meet him down by the river in the middle of the night tomorrow. That'll give us time to plan our route there and back to avoid cameras."

"It won't work. It's too risky. Even if we can't see cameras, we know damn well they're there. There has to be another way."

"Fine. Let's see what he wants first and go from there, all right? But I'm telling you, we're not putting up with his shit anymore."

They stood. She looped her arm with his again, and they headed towards the shops. Lately she'd got over her fear of being watched or followed, and maybe that was because she dragged Seven out with her more often than not these days, but tonight the feeling was back, likely because Mint had made an appearance and they'd be seeing him again soon.

She'd meant what she'd said about him, killing him, so long as it was as easy as pushing him in the river. Anything else regarding blood or whatever she couldn't handle. But then could she cope with her conscience pecking at her afterwards? The rest of her life was a long time to feel guilty for. Then there was the worry that everyone the police had spoken to would be looked at if his body washed up. Or would they look at Polly and wonder if she'd arranged for someone to kill him, despite her being inside?

They turned into an alley with a tall brick wall on the left and greenery on the right. It led to the delivery area behind the shops, and she was comforted by the fact that there must be CCTV there for when the lorries came, so if Mint thought to try anything, then it would be on camera.

The alley seemed really long as she stared down it, and she squeezed Seven's arm with hers to give herself a bit of reassurance that he was actually there and she wasn't on her own. They walked quickly, and it seemed he was as spooked as she was, a shudder going through him and transferring to her. She glanced at the trees and bushes, thinking that someone was going to jump out on them at any minute—after all, Mint had asked *them to come here, and it wouldn't surprise her one bit if he'd asked a dodgy mate along to give them a good going over.*

They reached the end and darted into the opening of the yard. The shops stood to the left, lights on in the flats above, which alleviated her nerves somewhat, because if she had to scream then someone might hear. A white Transit, a ghostly shape in the dark, had been backed close to the double wooden doors of what she'd worked out was the chippy. It couldn't be anything to do with Mint because there was a decal on the side with The Battered Cod *on it and a cartoon picture of a fish, but he could be hiding on the other side of it, waiting to pounce. She shivered and walked forward, tugging Seven to go with her, but he dug his heels in so she had to stop.*

It was either face whatever was behind the van or risk going back down the alley, and she knew which one she preferred. She'd rather have residents in the flats close by than feeling suffocated in the alley by the threat of someone who wanted to do them harm.

"Come on," she whispered. "The quicker we speak to him, the quicker we can go and get our chips."

"I'm not hungry anymore."

To be fair, neither was she, but she wasn't about to admit it; she went on at him enough about eating properly, and he was bound to mention it.

"He said he knows I spoke to Grace in the café. If that's all he wants to discuss, then we'll be fine."

They stepped forward, veering away from the van, walking along what she imagined was the bend of a rainbow until they got to see the other side. No Mint. She checked the shadows of the other doorways, and he wasn't there either. Moving along a bit so they reached the edge of the shops, she leaned to the right to look down the side in case he was hiding there. Nothing. A scrape from behind had her spinning round, letting go of Seven's arm, then grabbing it again as he turned around, too. She stared at Mint coming towards them, hands in his pockets. Did he have a weapon? Was he going to hurt them despite the CCTV?

To his rear stood a green bordered by what looked like a black impenetrable wall, but she worked out the tops of trees against a dark sky lit by what might be orange streetlamps behind them. Maybe there was a wall behind the trunks which was why no light pierced between.

She calculated escape routes, immediately discarding heading for those trees as scaling a wall wasn't something she thought she'd be able to do without Mint gripping her ankle just as she was about to pull herself over. There was the alley and an access road with a T-junction at the top, but the night cloaked anything else. The side of the shops was their best bet. It was so weird how she felt isolated and trapped at this moment, yet only metres away people were entering the chippy, the newsagent's, and the hairdresser's which stayed open late on a Friday.

It was okay. Provided they could run fast enough and he didn't have a gun to stop them escaping, she could get through this.

He'd moved onto the green, so she crossed the access road with Seven until they stood a few feet from him on the grass. She tried to work out whether he'd led them far enough into the dark that if something happened to them the cameras wouldn't pick it up, or had they been drawn over there so someone hiding in those trees had a clean shot? This was the sort of thing her imagination threw at her whenever it had the chance to run riot. She no longer had hallucinations brought on by drugs; her mind had decided to torment her instead.

She decided to take the upper hand here and act as though this wasn't bothering her. "So how come you know I met Grace? Have you been following me? Or did you get one of your scabby little drug customers to do it?"

"It doesn't matter how I know."

"How come it's taken you so long to get hold of me about it? That was a week ago. You have both of our phone numbers from when we rented off you. Why didn't you ring?"

Was it because he didn't want there to be a record of him contacting her?

"I've been busy," he said. "What did you talk about with her?"

"If you must know, she doesn't think it was you who stole the jewellery." She wanted to add *"even though you went to the house that night"*—but didn't because then he'd know **she'd** gone.

"Why would she even think I'd done it anyway?"

"Because you were there on the night she was taken from her house to the attic."

"How do you even know that?"

"She told me you were coming round for dinner."

He lifted a hand from his pocket, and she instinctively took a step back, panicking in case he had a knife, but he rubbed his palm over his forehead, closing his eyes for a moment.

"Jesus Christ, she wasn't meant to remember that. The medication was supposed to get rid of the memories of what went on just before she was taken."

"She doesn't think you had anything to do with her being in the attic, so stop worrying." Charlotte wasn't about to tell him that she thought Grace had been lying. "She's like us and wants to forget everything."

"What else did you talk about?"

"The weather."

"Seriously?"

"Seriously. I didn't know what else to chat about."

He spun round in a circle, staring at the inky sky, both hands in his pockets again. He looked at Seven as though he'd only just noticed him there. "And what about you? Have you been speaking to anybody about this?"

Charlotte laughed. "He only ever leaves the flat to go to work, and his job's in a little cubicle by himself, so who the hell would *he talk to?"*

"I don't know, maybe colleagues at lunchtime?" Mint's sarcasm hung heavy.

"I don't even like talking about it with her.*" Seven poked a finger in Charlotte's direction. "I wish I never knew about the murder. It's fucking with my head."*

Mint took a step forward, his own finger pointing. "Listen to me, you. If this fucking with your head ends up fucking with my life, you're going to regret it, so teach yourself that it didn't happen, you heard nothing, you saw nothing, and then everything will be all right."

Charlotte sensed Seven struggled with being near Mint, so she was going to have to take over. She stepped between them. "Leave him alone, he's got no intention of putting anyone in the shit because that would mean admitting he knew she was going to be killed, and there's no way he wants that coming out, so why don't you listen to me and piss off, stop harassing us, because we all want the same thing: to move on."

Mint sniffed, lowering his finger. "When I find out who the fuck phoned the police…"

A roll of anxiety flipped over in Charlotte's stomach, and Seven made a strangled noise. She elbowed him discreetly in the gut, warning him to keep it together at least until they'd walked away from Mint.

"Whoever it was, I'm grateful," Charlotte said.

"You what?" Mint laughed as if he couldn't believe what he'd just heard. "You're grateful?"

"Yes, because imagine if Polly had gone through with the murder, then the police would have looked at this a hell of a lot more closely, and you can bet things

would be different now. I doubt any of us three would be free."

"Don't say shit like that," Mint said. "Fucking tempting fate."

"Not if we don't ever get seen together again. You're tempting fate by making contact."

He didn't respond, just strutted away towards the trees.

Charlotte took the opportunity to tug Seven across the delivery yard and round the side of the shops, the light coming through the windows so welcome compared to the darkness they'd left behind. She took him into the chippy, bought their food, and handed him his package so he could carry it home under his spare arm the same as she'd do with hers; there was no way she was letting his other arm go. She sensed he was in the mood to bolt, so it was best she got him home.

They walked in silence, and when they rounded the corner into their street, Charlotte expected to see Mint standing there, but he wasn't. She turned into the communal front garden, her attention going straight to the top step in case there was a present there, but again, nothing to worry about. Once they were inside the safety of the flat, it occurred to her that Mint could have been distracting them behind the shops while someone broke in here. Looking for what, she didn't know, but seeing as her life had become a soap opera, anything was within the realms of possibility.

She left Seven to eat his chips on the sofa straight out of the packet, desperate to search the flat for any signs that an intruder had been in. She wouldn't put it past Mint to have cameras put in, and she slumped her shoulders at the thought of trying to find them if they were those really small ones. Nothing felt out of place or odd anyway, so she put it down to her imagination again, sitting beside Seven to eat her sausage and chips.

Chapter Twenty-Four

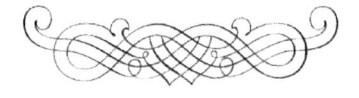

Sharon felt a hell of a lot better knowing that Mint had died. She'd leave the kids to stay with their dad until the agreed time, no point in upsetting them, and besides, she had something she needed to do. George had put the idea into her head, and while she'd agreed that they'd go and see her mother for her and explain things, she really should do it herself. She owed her parents that much.

It had been years since she'd stepped foot in the house she'd grown up in, and she wasn't sure how she was going to feel when she did it again. Was everything the same, or had it changed beyond recognition? Would it still feel like home or a stranger's house? Had Sharon created distance between herself and her mother that could never be fixed? Was it going to be awkward when they spoke, or would Mum forgive her no matter what? She didn't want to be in a situation where unspoken words lingered, dying to be spoken but neither of them willing to be the first to say what needed to be said. Maybe she should just go in there, apologise, and take any recriminations on the chin.

She walked down the familiar street, a slew of memories hitting her one after the other: playing out on the road; going round to her best friend's next door to play in her Wendy house; French skipping with elastic around her ankles. Fucking hell, the nostalgia was heavy. She strode up the garden path, and for a moment it felt like she'd never been away, but then the guilt crashed in to remind her that she had, for far too long.

She was a terrible daughter.

As usual in the summer, the door was slightly open—Mum always did that in case a neighbour needed to pop in, and it was nice to see she could still do that in this day and age, where doors were locked more often than not, people shunning their neighbours through fear of getting their heads bitten off. No one seemed to have the time to make friends anymore. Sharon certainly hadn't.

She pushed the door wider and planted one foot inside, the floor creaking with her weight like it always used to. Mum was cooking something, maybe a stew, and the scent of bread lingered. Did she still use the bread maker? Sharon entered fully, shutting the door behind her—she didn't need an audience for what she was about to say, and if Julie from three doors down had seen Sharon coming, she'd make no bones about walking in to get the gossip, and, most likely, give Sharon a dressing-down, one she deserved without question.

Mum appeared in the doorway to the kitchen at the end of the hall, her hair silver instead of brown with speckles of grey. She'd put it up on top of her head in a scruffy bun. The wrinkles on her face were so much more pronounced now, and Sharon had to acknowledge that she had probably put them there, she had made them score deep. The guilt of it brought a lump to her throat. Mum continued to stare, flour on her fingertips and tiny clumps of pastry where she must have been rubbing in the butter.

So many unresolved feelings swirled through Sharon, sentences without full stops on the end, and that was all her fault.

"Charlotte!" Mum said, sounding pleased but the same time shocked, surprised, disbelieving.

All the words Sharon had rehearsed formed a scribble of threads that she couldn't untangle. Her eyes burned from tears. "Hello, Mum."

"Oh, Jesus Christ, come here, will you?"

Sharon rushed into her arms, and all of the tension and years of problems faded away. They always had when Mum cuddled her, and this feeling was the one thing she'd missed the most, knowing she was safe and that Mum had her back.

"I don't need to know anything if you don't want to tell me." Mum stroked Sharon's hair. "I'm just glad you're back, that's all that matters."

Mum had a fancy coffee machine where she had to grind the beans. The smell of a fresh brew mixed with that of the cherry pie she'd been making when Sharon had turned up. Once Mum had finished making it, Sharon had encouraged her to tell her what had been going on while she'd been gone; she'd launch into her own story soon enough, but for now she just wanted to catch up. Sharon had asked her not to phone Dad to come home from work. Not yet. She couldn't cope with both of them crying.

Mum looked like she'd battled through far too many storms without an umbrella. "I can still remember the first time I made that cherry pie."

Sharon smiled. "We'd gone to Nan's. I wish we could rewind time. Go back to when I was a kid so I could make different decisions."

"Do you regret making the decision to leave?"

"No. I did it to keep you and Dad safe." Sharon rubbed her finger around the rim of her cup, remembering how as a child she'd done it with a glass and it had made the *whoo* sound of a ghost.

"*What?*"

Sharon told her everything then, surprising herself with the complete honesty, trying not to notice Mum's wince when she mentioned taking cocaine. It had to be a difficult one, that, to hear that your child had gone down one of the paths you'd warned them against.

"I'm sorry you went through that," Mum said. "I suppose I ought to be truthful with you now. I thought it was to do with a man, but not in the way you just told me. I thought you'd got swept up by someone who was controlling and needed you to cut ties with us so he could really get his claws in. I was angry at you for choosing him over us, and there were times when I needed you, when your dad got poorly—it was his appendix, nothing to worry about now—and I missed you more than I ever thought possible."

"I'm so bloody sorry. Now I'm on the other side of it, I can see it was wrong to run away, especially because he'd gone to prison, but I convinced myself he had fingers in lots of pies and he'd send someone to come after me."

"I saw it in the paper and had no idea the Grace thing was anything to do with you."

"Why would you? The Charlotte you knew, the good girl you'd brought up, would never have even contemplated sitting with an old lady knowing she was going to die."

"It was the drugs, it had to be. They messed with your mind."

Sharon looked across at her, eyes stinging again. "Maybe, but perhaps I ought to accept the fact that I was a cow during that time."

"You weren't your best self, but it's okay, I'll help you through it. Where's that Mint man now? How come you were able to visit me?"

"This is the bit you might not like."

Previous to this, Sharon had got up to the part of the story where she'd split up with her ex and had chosen to remain single. Mum had been delighted at the idea of grandsons, and Sharon had promised to bring them round at the weekend for Sunday dinner then a bit of trifle.

"I should imagine you've told me the worst already, haven't you?" Mum said.

"Depends what you think about leaders."

"Oh…"

"There's still a fair bit of the story to tell."

"I'm listening."

Sharon explained about Mint's reappearance outside the Shiny Fork, then what had happened after that. Mum's kitchen seemed to disappear around her, and whatever was going on beyond this house became insignificant as she recounted what George had told her about Mint's death. She had to backtrack a couple of times to fill Mum in on how she'd even known the twins' phone number to ask for help, but now she was drawing her tale to a close, she wondered how she'd come out of it with her sanity.

"It's what leaders do," Mum said. "It was out of your hands. Don't blame yourself that he's dead."

Sharon looked at her, unable to tell another lie. "But I'm *happy* he's dead. It means I'm safe now, and more importantly, my boys are safe."

For the first time since she'd walked out of this house years ago, hope fizzled inside her, obliterating the darkness of guilt that had always been present regarding their estrangement. Life was never going to be easy, not for Sharon, she'd long ago accepted she'd face challenges every step of the way, but she had Mum on her side now, and Dad once he got home, although she'd leave it up to Mum to tell him everything that had gone on. Going through all that again would be too exhausting.

Mum cut a triangle of cherry pie and put it on a small plate, pushing it across the table towards Sharon. "Shall I ring your dad now?"

Sharon nodded.

"He's going to be so pleased you've come back."

Sharon imagined him getting in the car, thinking that at last he'd have the chance to thump the man who they'd assumed had taken their daughter away, but that man was now dead, and good riddance to the bastard.

If he had a grave she'd dance on it.

Chapter Twenty-Five

There was no way this was supposed to have happened. Charlotte shouldn't be staring at a bold black headline on her phone that had changed her life completely in the time it had taken for her to read it.

ELDERLY LADY IN ATTIC CASE FOUND DEAD

It felt like her bedroom tilted, a sharp lurch to starboard on the ultra-choppy sea of the life she'd now have to navigate. Her first thought was that it must be Grace and she'd been killed, either by Polly arranging the hit from prison or Mint doing it because of the discussion at the back of the shops last night. It was more likely to be him, going to the assisted-living place and…doing what? She needed to read the article to find out.

> Grace Peterson, 84, was found in bed at her assisted-living, ground-floor flat at 8 a.m. by one of the care workers, Jasmin Evans, 24. Mrs Peterson's throat had been cut with her own knife taken from a block in her kitchen. Her bedroom window was open.
>
> When asked how someone had been able to enter an assisted-living facility without any alarms going off or someone seeing the intruder, the manager, Vincent Watson, 53, said the police were looking into it and he declined to comment further.

Mrs Peterson had recently been kidnapped from her house and taken to an attic where she had been visited and kept alive for some time with a view to ending her life on an undisclosed date. An anonymous phone call to the police alerted the authorities to the situation. The caller has never been found. Police urge them to get in contact again now that Mrs Peterson is deceased.

Charlotte fought against throwing up. Jesus Christ, this was worse than what her imagination had come up with. Yes, she'd thought about Mint murdering the old dear, but not slicing her throat. That poor woman finding the body. All that blood… Charlotte shivered, a sense of suffocation coming over her, claustrophobia that the proverbial walls were closing in. That she might be next.

They had to get out of here. Move away.

She checked her bank account. She had enough to pay her half of the bills and rent, plus there was some left over for the deposit to rent a room in a shared house, which would be so much cheaper than what she was shelling out for now. She'd have to factor in the cost of changing her name, but if she didn't go to the pub tonight, as she'd planned, then that would save her a few quid.

She glanced at the clock. Ten-fifteen. She doubted Seven would be awake, but this was definitely not something she could keep from him. She left her room to go to his, tapping on the door and opening it without waiting for him to say she could enter. The smell hit her again, the air so thick with body heat that she wanted to heave. As usual, she left the door open then sat on the end of his bed in direct line with the fresh air coming in. She shook his shoulder to wake him up, and he shot upright, fist swinging. She reared back so she wasn't hit, holding her arms up to shield herself.

"Fucking hell, it's only me," she barked.

He lowered his hands, still in a sleepy daze, and stared at her as if he'd never seen her before in his life. Slowly, he came back to the land of the living, blinking then knuckling his eyes. "What…what time is it?"

"Just after ten, and before you ask, it's Saturday."

"Right. What do you want?"

"There's bad news."

"Oh God, don't…"

*"I mean **really** bad news."*

"I don't think I can cope with any more."

His gaze flickered to his bedside table and a packet of antidepressants—Charlotte recognised the name of them because her mother used to take them. He looked at her again, and she tried to read his eyes, his expression, but he was just so blank, no life in him, the spark put out.

"Don't even think of doing that," she said to him. "It wouldn't be fair because it's me who'd find you, and what about your mum and dad and your brothers and sisters, how they'd feel with you gone."

"I'm one of seven; I was always the odd one out, so I doubt very much they'd give a shit. None of them hardly talk to me."

"Do you talk to them? Send messages and stuff?"

"No."

"Well then, it goes both ways."

"I didn't want to bother them with all…this." He glanced at the tablets again. "They'd take the piss, say I'm not a man because I'm finding it hard to cope and I need medication."

"I'd care if you weren't here," she said. "Even if you are a mopey shit."

At least she'd got a smile out of him, which was more than he'd been willing to give lately. She wished she didn't have to shatter his world, but it was best they were both in the loop with anything regarding

Grace and Mint. So she told him what had happened, watching him carefully, how he reacted. He flinched at first—the mention of Grace being dead had done that—and then he covered his face with his hands when she told him how she'd died.

He scraped them down his face so his eyes looked like a basset hound's for a second. "So did someone break in or was her window already open?"

"It didn't say, just that the window was open."

"It has to be Mint."

"That's exactly what I thought. If he didn't do it then he got someone else to. I'm more inclined to think he got a scrote to do it so he could make sure he had an alibi."

"When did it happen?"

"No idea. I assume it was in the middle of the night."

"Does he even have a wife or someone who'd be willing to give him an alibi?"

"That's something else I don't know, but maybe it's something we should *know. He's been following us, so why shouldn't we follow him?"*

"Bloody hell, Char…"

"Let's face it, we know sod all about him apart from the fact that he's apparently an estate agent, he rents rooms out to tenants who he also sells drugs to. That's

it. Where does he live? Has he got a wife? Don't you think it's better that we know our enemy?"

"What did you say that for? Do you think he's going to come after us next?"

Charlotte had to be careful how she answered this one. His glances at the tablets had worried her.

"If he did then it's going to look really suspicious, isn't it. We were both spoken to about the kidnap because we lived in the house at the time she was there and just happened to move out on the day of the tip-off. If we end up dead, they're going to look straight at Mint, so no, I don't think he'll come after us, all right?"

"All right." He puffed air out, his cheeks inflated. "So how are we going to go about this then?"

"What, you're actually going to get off your arse and do something?" She smiled to file the edges off the barb.

"I've had enough. Something has to be done. We do what you suggested and make him have an accident, or we find something else on him that can get him put away."

"What do you mean, find something? He's a drug dealer, for fuck's sake."

"Yeah, but we don't know where he stores the drugs."

"I'm not sure following him around in my car is going to be a good idea. He knows what I drive, he'd spot it."

"I've got enough saved to hire one for the week."

"Fine, then we'll go to the house tonight because we know he's always there on a Saturday to hand out the drugs. We'll follow him after."

"Unless in the meantime he gets arrested for the murder."

"That would be nice, but the way things have gone for us so far, I can't see us getting that lucky, can you?"

The hire car, an inconspicuous silver Ford, had comfortable seats, and the heater worked a treat compared to her car. They currently sat outside the house, waiting for Mint to turn up. It was closing in on nine, and there he was, like clockwork, slotting his motor into a gap outside the property, getting out and letting himself in. She imagined him continuing the same routine he always had, knocking on each individual door to sell his wares, trying to get the tenants to buy more than they could afford so they owed him. She thought about that greasy-haired bloke who now lived in her old room. He looked the type to get so in debt with Mint that he risked a good kicking if he didn't pay up. She felt sorry for him, for anyone hooked on drugs, because what started out as a bit of fun could so quickly turn into your life coming off the tracks.

Ten minutes passed without Charlotte and Seven speaking, the usual these days because he barely spoke unless she initiated the conversation. Now that he was actually being proactive, hiring the car and being prepared to part with his own money for it, that was proof enough for her that he'd really had enough. Maybe he'd come to another crossroads in his journey of depression where he could choose to continue going down into the dark well or he could reach for the circle of sunlight above and let it warm his frozen-with-lethargy bones.

She was proud of him.

Mint came out of the house, dragging her attention away from thoughts of Seven. He got into his car and drove off, Charlotte easing out of their spot to follow. He next stopped three streets away at another Victorian. He entered using a key.

"Bloody hell, he must be loaded," Seven said.

"Hmm. But how can we be surprised when he sells drugs? Being an estate agent means he'll have the pick

of houses as soon as they come on the market. Knowing him he's probably got about five that he rents out to the desperate fuckers."

"Makes you wonder how he met Polly in the first place. Was she on drugs or did she come in to buy property?"

"God knows, but if he was seeing Polly, maybe he doesn't have a wife. Or I suppose he could have been seeing Polly on the side."

"And now it's come out that they were having an affair, he might not have a wife at all now."

"She could have fucked off."

"Took the kids."

"Picked a nice cottage and bought a dog."

"Cleaning the windows every week."

"Hanging the washing out in the garden."

They laughed—God, it was so nice to talk how they used to. All right, it had been when they were high and they'd made up lives for people, but just then she'd had a glimpse of Seven definitely letting the sun shine on him.

"It'll be okay somehow," she said. "We'll get him arrested or something."

Mint came out, their conversation cut short. They followed him to yet another house, the same routine happening, but the next time they moved off he drove to a row of garages. If Charlotte had turned in behind him he would have known something was going on, so she had to keep going as though she hadn't been tailing him. She parked in a nearby street, and they got out, scurrying towards the garages surrounded by a horseshoe of trees.

They hid behind a trunk each. Mint came out of one of the garages, light spilling onto the tarmac in front and illuminating the back of his car. The boot was open, the tops of cardboard boxes just about visible. He took them out and into the garage one by one, seeming to struggle despite his size. She bet they weighed heavy with bricks of cocaine or heroin, because he very rarely sold weed.

He locked up the garage, shut the boot, and drove away.

Charlotte stared across at Seven who leaned his back on the trunk and stared at the star-speckled sky.

"What are you thinking?" she asked.

"That we should wait for a bit and then go over there and see what number garage it is. You're going to need that when you phone the police."

"Oh, so it's me who's doing it, is it."

"Yeah, because I'll only go and fuck it up. I'll get flustered and shit."

She couldn't argue with that, but still, it was annoying that he'd assumed it would be her. Maybe he thought because he'd shelled out for the hire car that he'd done his part. Cheeky bastard, considering what she'd done to get the deposit money for the flat.

She leaned on a tree herself and shoved her hands in her pockets, thinking about how she could contact the police. There was no way she was going back to the bookies, so she'd have to look up where there were still pay phones in the area. It was cheaper than buying a burner phone or a new SIM that she could throw away afterwards. She'd also look up the number of the local police station this time—this wasn't exactly a nine-nine-nine situation.

With everything sorted in her mind, she said, "Let's go and have a look, then. Hoods up, heads down, and no talking until we get back to the car."

They trudged over some mulchy ground and onto the tarmac. She glanced to the left as they passed the garage Mint had gone into. A plaque on the white-painted bricks in between doors had the number six on it. She nudged Seven to let him know they needed to go back the way they'd come.

In the car, she let out a long breath, telling herself to calm down. She looked up where the nearest payphone was but didn't want to take the car there in case it got spotted on cameras. She drove away and parked three streets from the pub down a lane that led to some scrubland.

"This is a bit creepy," Seven muttered.

"Better than the car being spotted on someone's doorbell camera, though, eh?"

"I suppose."

"There's no suppose about it. We don't want this car being flagged up. It'll be traced to the fact that you hired it."

She brought Google Maps up on her phone so she could plot her route. Thankfully there was a park she could cut across, then come out of an alley between houses, crossing the street to the pub directly opposite.

She told Seven what she was doing. "Sit tight until I get back."

She left the car, taking her own advice—hood up, head down—and ran across the park. It was so dark she scared herself, convinced someone followed, their heavy footsteps thudding, but it was just her own reverberating through her body. She burst out of the alley, stopping at the kerb to catch her breath then darting across the road, entering the pub, never so thankful to see the payphone right there in the entryway. There was another door to go into the pub itself, so unless somebody opened it to exit, she was anonymous here. She quickly put a pound coin on top of the phone casing, ready for when she needed it, then brought the local station's number up on her mobile. She pushed the metal buttons of the payphone and pressed the pound coin into the slot as soon as the call was answered.

If this didn't get Mint put in prison and out of their hair, she'd have to concoct a plan B.

Chapter Twenty-Six

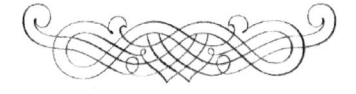

Henry Greaves' wealth was reflected in his house, all the mod cons, expensive granite on the floor instead of carpet, tasteful artwork. The place had the air of the clinical about it, hospital-like in that it smelled of disinfectant and the walls were white, but there was a fair bit of bling going on with chandeliers and ornaments, perhaps courtesy of his wife who was much younger than him.

They'd gathered in his 'orangery', which to George was just a plain old fucking conservatory, no fancy names needed, and there wasn't an orange in sight, so what was that all about?

Everyone had a small whisky and a square of ice in crystal tumblers. Old man Greaves and Nathaniel sat on two of the comfortable leather recliners, George and Greg on the matching sofa opposite. Greaves' wife, a blonde called Karen, hovered in the corner watering some hanging plants.

"Why don't you fuck off, darlin'," Greaves said to her. "This is men's business."

Misogynistic twat.

She tottered off in her high heels, leaving the door that led into the house open.

"Door!" Greaves shouted.

Footsteps tapped where she ran to do his bidding, then the door closed.

"A nosy girl, but she gives a good blow job." Greaves cackled.

Nathaniel didn't look impressed.

"What can I do for you?" Greaves asked.

George had been intending to ask either him or Nathaniel to drop by and explain things to Ashley for them, but he'd changed his mind. "We'd like permission to speak to one of your residents."

"Something to do with this Mint geezer Nathaniel's been looking into for you?" the old boy asked.

"Yeah. We want to assure her she's got nothing to worry about."

Greaves pinched his chin, studying George. "Mint's been dispatched?"

"Something like that."

"I had a feeling that would happen. You were too interested in him. I have to say I'm not too happy at finding out what he's been up to on my Estate. I'm out of pocket, he didn't pay me any protection money, and you two got rid of him before I had the chance to ask him for it."

George had met many men like Greaves, always out for money, and to be fair, what he'd said was correct. "How much are we talking?"

"Fifty grand should do it."

Fuck me sideways. "Twenty, take it or leave it. One of our men will come round with it."

Greaves sipped his drink. "I'll look forward to seeing him."

"We'd like a receipt."

"Fine by me. It'll say I bought a car off you."

"Right."

Nathaniel must have sensed the tension, so he changed the subject, talking about the winery they were going to buy in Italy.

"He's taking my Karen over there soon," Greaves said, "because she'll be living out there permanently, running the business."

George downed his whisky and stood—he had no need to listen to tripe about the wife. "Thanks for the drink."

Nathaniel got to his feet at the same time as Greg. "I'll see you out."

They left the elder man, walking through the pristine house past Karen who eyed them up and down. Out on the gravel driveway, George and Greg about to get into the BMW, Nathaniel hovered as though he wanted to say something but didn't know if he should.

"What's the matter?" George asked.

"I need your help," he whispered then glanced around to let them know they might be being watched—or heard. "What my dad said about sending Karen to Italy. That's not really happening in the way he implied."

"So what *is* really happening?" Although George had a bloody good idea; it had suddenly hit him, the undercurrent, Greaves calling her nosy. She was being sent abroad to die.

"He wants me to kill her while we're over there. Make it look like she drowned in the pool while drunk so the authorities there are satisfied. As for here, he'll retain the lie that she's alive and working in Italy."

"Why is he doing this?"

"He thinks she's working for someone who wants to know his business."

"Who?"

"I don't know, he won't say, but she listens a lot, she knows too much—he says it's like she's spying on him. I can't do it, I can't go there with her knowing she's going to snuff it."

"You care about her."

"Yes. She's been nothing but loyal to him as far as I'm concerned, and if she *is* working for someone, then I think whoever they are should be rooted out and held to account. Dad thinks it's the drugs they're interested in. Karen keeps asking where they come from."

"Maybe she's just curious."

"Maybe."

"So what do you want us to do?"

"Stop the order for her death."

"Look, there's not a lot we can do other than have a little chat with him. Let us have a think about it and get back to you. We've got to go and see Mint's wife."

"Okay. We've got a bit of time. We're not supposed to be going to Italy until next month."

George and Greg got in the car and buckled up.

"What did you make of that then?" George asked.

"She was definitely trying to listen in until he sent her away."

"Hmm. Interesting."

Chapter Twenty-Seven

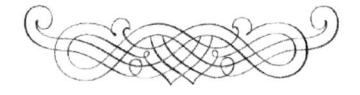

Sometimes, Sharon allowed herself to think back to her time as Charlotte, when her life had been so fraught with tension and her imagination tortured her on the daily. For a long time she'd managed to completely ignore the person she used to be, and the fact that Charlotte had existed at all, and that her parents probably wondered where she'd disappeared

to, why she was moving on and that she didn't want to have any contact anymore.

It was a horrible thing to do, she knew that now she'd become a parent herself. She couldn't imagine her boys telling her they were cutting ties and she'd never see them again.

Mint had gone to prison for the possession of drugs he had yet to pay for, and so the rumours had said, his dealers weren't happy. They were after anyone who had any information, and if they found the person who'd tipped off the police, then blood would be shed. It hadn't been put quite like that on social media, the threat had been implied, but she'd got the gist and, paranoid that someone would eventually remember seeing her bursting out of the pub where she'd used the phone, and somebody recognising her from the description… She couldn't stand for her parents to be dragged into it if they knew where she'd gone. At least if they didn't, they couldn't tell anyone anything.

She'd been a wicked person to leave that part of London to start again on the Cardigan Estate. Leave her parents to deal with any aftermath should the dealers discover who their daughter was and what she'd done. As Charlotte she'd been a selfish person, although she'd been one who was trying to redeem herself by saving Grace. That hadn't worked out too well in the end, Grace dying anyway, but at least she'd tried to put things right. Only to possibly put her parents in the line of fire with her disappearance, when to be honest, seeing as the police had never discovered who'd made that phone call about the drugs, she could have stayed living in the flat with Seven.

But they'd both had to get away. Maybe he felt the same as she had, that making a giant slice down that section of her life, to cut it off completely from who she was going to become, was the best thing to do. If Seven hadn't given himself a new name and moved away, she honestly thought he'd have tipped those tablets down his throat. As for her, if she'd remained in the same area she would have been on constant alert. At least on Cardigan, with her hair changed and the extra weight she'd put on having her kids, she looked nothing like Charlotte.

If she made friends with anyone, she told them her parents had disowned her for having children out of wedlock—that way she didn't have to speak about her past because she made out it was too painful. Even her ex thought that was what had happened. She'd conveniently reshaped her life into something completely different to Charlotte's when she'd become Sharon.

The summer evening was drawing in, and she sat in her council flat, lonely now the kids had gone to bed. Her time with their father had lasted long enough for two pregnancies back to back, then he'd copped off with another woman. She couldn't fault him on how he helped her to look after their children, though. He had them overnight for half of the week—probably so he didn't have to pay child support—and he took them nice places, like Chessington World of Adventures, and the cinema was a regular thing, followed by McDonald's or Burger King.

No air was coming through at all, even with the balcony doors open. She'd done a load of washing, the kids' uniforms drying out on an airer, and she stared into the middle distance, sweating and hot—and getting more and more pissed off at the smell of weed coming from the flat next door. She'd had a word with the resident about it before. He seemed to be deliberately blowing the smoke across to her balcony, so maybe he was sitting out there, but her irritable mood meant she wasn't prepared to put up with it this evening.

She got up and stormed round there, knocking on the door.

The man answered. Big. Black. Although he didn't look scary. Mint was more frightening to her. It was all in the eyes. You could tell a lot from those.

"If you don't stop blowing that shit through those fucking balcony doors so the stink comes round to my flat, I'm going to phone the police." Of course she wouldn't be bloody doing that, the last people she wanted to see were the police, but maybe the threat of it would make him think twice.

He smiled at her. Held the joint up. "You might feel better if you smoke some. You should live by the mantra, 'Don't worry, be happy'."

Smoke some? Jesus, that was the last thing she wanted to do. She'd get hooked on the stuff, although to be fair to herself, she still smoked fags, but only a few. Maybe that's why she was so annoyed, deep down. Could she be jealous that he could smoke weed and she couldn't? Or she'd chosen not to because she knew she had an addictive personality and couldn't risk it, especially now she had the kids? And as for him saying don't worry, be happy…

"How can I fucking do that when I've got mouths to feed and bills to pay, eh? I've got my washing out on my balcony, and my kids are going to smell like pot when they go to school tomorrow because that smoke keeps going all over their uniforms. It isn't right, what

you're doing." Oh, what a hypocrite she was. Sniffing cocaine wasn't right either, yet she'd been happy enough to do it.

"I'll stop it after I finish this one, all right?"

She believed him, yet said, "You'd better."

She stalked back to her door, giving him a glare when she got there, tutting as though she had every right to judge him, when in fact, she had no right at all. She went inside, listening out for if her shouting had woken up the kids, but all was quiet. They were going to their dad's after school tomorrow for the next couple of nights, so she'd get the flat cleaned from top to bottom, something she did a lot of while they were away so it stopped her being reminded of how lonely she was.

But she'd chosen to walk away from Charlotte's life and into Sharon's so only had herself to blame.

<hr />

The next day, with the kids at school along with their backpacks containing clothing for their stay at their father's, Sharon had returned home intending to tackle the housework, but she'd got hungry and looked in the cupboards and the fridge, finding fuck all there. She was going to have to go to the bloody supermarket, wasn't she, get a few bits in to stock up, something she didn't relish doing. She always felt too exposed with the amount of people who were also there—maybe it was irrational, but she usually got paranoid that someone from where she used to live would be over this part of London and recognise her, despite the state she was in now, with saggy tits and a fat arse. She doubted even Seven would know who she was. He'd likely walk straight past her in the street. Would it be the same the other way around? Hadn't he mentioned growing a beard?

She collected her handbag and left the flat, intending to get something nice to eat from the café down the road, seeing as she'd just got her benefits through. She definitely wasn't the type anymore to go and get her nails done as soon as she got some cash, but she did like a good round of toast and a cup of tea that she hadn't had to make herself. It was her one treat if you didn't count the couple of packets of cigarettes she bought a month, and she needed to stop that because they were so expensive.

The heat hit her as she closed the front door. It was going to be another hot one. Maybe she'd get lucky and one of those cheap fans she'd seen in the supermarket would still be there this week. She hadn't had the money last time, and she really needed a fan for her bedroom as she'd given the other one to her boys.

The bloke from next door came out of his flat. Embarrassment fluttered inside her. It was different when you saw someone after all the anger had dissolved. Maybe she ought to be nice to him. She'd got so caught up in how crap her life was compared to what she thought it would be, that she was sometimes sour and bitter towards people, as though it was **their** *fault she'd made the decisions she had. And what was it she'd told herself all those years ago? Be a better person. Be good so that karma didn't come to get her. She hadn't escaped it so far, what with the ex fucking off with someone else, but she deserved to be punished.*

She couldn't blame him, not really. When she'd met him she'd not long become Sharon and hadn't known who she'd wanted to be. She'd still lugged Charlotte's baggage around, even if it was just mental suitcases in her head, and she hadn't exactly been consistent in her moods. She'd struggled with the guilt from leaving her parents behind, plus wondering what Seven was up to and whether he was still alive. He could have succumbed to those tablets for all she knew.

She stopped herself from going down that maudlin route by concentrating on locking her door.

"Wagwan," the man said.

She smiled, preparing to launch into nice mode. Come on, it wasn't that hard, she did it every bloody day when she dropped the kids off, speaking to the mums in the playground. "Morning. Off somewhere nice?"

Did she really think a weed-smoking man was off to do something nice? He could be just like the others who'd rented the rooms in Mint's house, off his tree all the time. But she shouldn't judge—you could smoke weed and be a completely lovely person. She was still learning this new path she'd put herself on, but it was no excuse to think such mean and twisted things about people she didn't even know. He could think she was an unattractive blimp, never once thinking that she used to be attractive and slim. He could be reading her book cover just as spitefully as she'd read his.

"Just to meet a friend," *he said.* "You?"

"Food shopping." *She took a breath. She was going to have to apologise to him. She really hadn't been herself when she'd stormed round there last night, but more than the kids smelling of pot at school, she was worried that her ex might think she was on drugs and try to get the children taken away from her. They were the only bright spot in her world, and the thought of being without them…well, it was unthinkable. She couldn't bring it to mind without crying.* "Thanks for *not…you know, not having a go at me when I spoke to you last night."* Had she sounded sincere enough?

"S'all right."

Going by his expression, it seemed he'd taken it in the spirit she'd intended. Or had she misread things? There was something about the slump of his shoulders that indicated things might not be all rosy in his garden.

Join the club.

She was going to press him, see if he wanted to open up. God knew she could do with a friend, and maybe he needed one, too. They could prop each other up. "You look like you've got the weight of the world on your shoulders."

"I've got a weight, yeah. Nothing that can be done about it, though."

She was right, he did *have shit going on, but that didn't mean he wanted to talk to her about it. They were strangers. He didn't know her and she didn't know him, so why the fuck would he trust her with any of his problems? She'd never tell him about hers, who she'd been and what she'd got up to, not even if she'd known him for years. The only person she'd ever discuss it with was Seven, and even though they had a burner phone each, it was only supposed to be for emergencies. They'd gone their separate ways, knowing they'd never see each other again unless the shit hit the fan.*

"Something can always be done," she said and doubted he'd realise how true she'd discovered that was. Things could be so, so bad, with seemingly no way out, no chink of light at the end of that bastard tunnel, but there was always an alternative. Look at what she'd been involved with, how defeated she'd felt at times, how Seven had struggled so much with everything, yet something had still been done.

She felt so sorry for this fella that she blurted, "I've got time for a coffee if you need to talk."

He stared at her with his eyebrows raised as though he couldn't believe what had just come out of her mouth, especially after the way she'd had a go at him last night.

He checked the time on his phone. "I can't let my friend down."

He had a little think, and she really hoped he'd say yes. He was a bit of all right, actually, and in another lifetime she might have tried her luck with him, but he was a lot younger than her, and she was well aware of what she looked like these days, how there was no way he'd find her attractive. If she did hint at fancying him he'd probably laugh his head off at her, a big ouch she really didn't need.

"Fuck, okay," he said.

Surprised he'd agreed, because she wasn't exactly the approachable type anymore, someone anyone would want to have a coffee with, she went along the walkway ahead of him, down the stairs that smelled of urine, yet another feature of her life that showed her exactly where she'd been and what she now put up with.

She was going to end up feeling sorry for herself again, so she brushed thoughts of piss aside and walked out onto the path. The sun had been bloody hot lately, and it wouldn't be long before she was sweating like a pig. Bloody hell, maybe she ought to go for long walks every day after she'd dropped the kids off at school, and change her diet, do something about herself before it really was too late.

She walked around the corner, the café in sight.

"Bloody hot, isn't it?" she said to him, and it reminded her of when she'd spoken to Grace about the weather.

"Much hotter where I'm from. This is nothing."

This was her chance to try and be more friendly, to be interested in someone other than herself and her own problems. She didn't bother to sound interested to the women at school because she had a feeling that making friends with them would be a big mistake. They gossiped a lot, tried to draw her into slagging other mothers off, but she always kept her mouth shut. But as much as she wished it wasn't true, blokes were different, so maybe having a male friend was the best way to go.

"Where are you from?" she asked.

"Jamaica."

"Are you here on holiday?"

"Yeah."

What she wouldn't give to go on a holiday to Jamaica. Her ex went abroad a lot, not something they'd ever done as a couple. Money had been tight when they'd got together, and he'd wanted her to stay at home rather than go to work when she'd had children. She'd been happy to do it because she'd loved being close to her babies all day, but he'd grown more ambitious, climbing the ladder, and just after the point he'd had an affair, when he'd moved out, he'd got a bloody pay rise which would have meant she could have gone to Spain and Turkey and all those places the new woman enjoyed.

The one thing Sharon didn't do was blame her. She'd been lied to, told that he was separated from his wife. Bloody bastard.

She pushed into the café and stomped to the top corner by the till, flumping down and letting out a sigh, glad of the air-conditioning. He sat opposite her, making no move to look at the menu, which had her wondering whether he was skint. She ordered for them, toast and tea.

"Assuming that's what you want," she said.

He took a tenner out of his wallet and put it on the table. So he wasn't skint, then. She frowned, annoyed at herself that she hadn't read him right. That's what happened when you became so self-absorbed and removed yourself from society as much as you could. You forgot how to read expressions and body language.

"You mentioned you had it tough," he said. "Last night."

Had he mistaken her frown as a question as to why he'd offered to pay?

"Oh yeah. Thanks."

The server walked away, so Sharon leaned back and folded her arms.

Come on, you can do this. Bring some of Charlotte's spirit and confidence back. Pretend he's Seven. It'll be easier to talk to him that way.

"So what's up with you, then?" she asked.

"It's not something I can talk about—not just in public but with anyone."

She knew how that went, how there was no way you could talk to someone, even though you were desperate to. She'd been lucky, though. She'd had Seven. This poor bastard might not have anyone. And he could be into all sorts, stuff she really didn't want to get involved with, but she'd brought him to the café now, so she was going to have to continue to play the part.

"So you're into dodgy shit, are you?" she asked.

"You could say that."

That had surprised her. She hadn't expected him to admit to it. "And?"

"I want to get out."

"So get out." She'd said that as though it was simple, when she knew full well that it might not be. But he wasn't to know what she'd been through, and she had no intention of revealing it, so she had to behave like anybody else would in this situation and answer accordingly.

"It's not that easy."

I know. *"Oh."*

"It's gang related."

Oh shit, this was worse than she'd thought. Did she really want to get involved with somebody like that? But what if he just needed a helping hand? And what if this was her big chance to prove to herself that she really was a good person? She could help him escape, to get away, although how she'd do that without her kids being in danger she didn't know. It wasn't just a case of thinking about herself anymore, she had her little boys. Oh God, she really didn't know what to do for the best.

"Ouch," she said. "Erm, are you doing gang-related shit while here on holiday?"

"Um, yeah?"

Oh dear. She doubted very much he knew about the leaders if he was fucking about on Cardigan doing God knew what. "Then watch your back, okay?"

His eyebrows drew together. "What do you mean?"

"Have you heard about London leaders?"

He shook his head. So she told him all about them, and it looked like he had no clue, and also that he was angry he hadn't been in the know.

"Shit," *he said.*

Because of his intention to get out of the gang, she couldn't let him walk out of here not knowing the full story. "There are spies everywhere, just so you know."

He eyed her. "Are you one of them?"

She laughed. "If I was, I wouldn't be skint, would I. You get paid for being a grass."

"Will you grass on me?" *he asked her.*

She could, she'd get a payout from The Brothers if she told them the Jamaican next door was into some dodgy crap, but it didn't feel right. "Nah."

"Why not?"

She shrugged. "I sense we're kindred spirits. Both down on our luck—or down on something anyway. And you want to get out of whatever it is you're in, so you can't be all that bad." She stopped talking; the server had arrived, putting their tea and toast down. She waited for her to go and then said, "The twins will probably help you."

She wasn't sure if they would or not, but wasn't it worth a try?

He didn't seem convinced. "They're not going to help me, not after what I've done."

What the hell had *he done? Surely it couldn't be as bad as being involved in a murder plot, keeping an old lady company, going to her house to feed a dead budgie and then stealing her jewellery. Phoning the police to grass on Mint—twice—then running away with her new name to start again.*

No, it couldn't be as bad as that.

She poured tea. He looked at his phone, maybe to see what time it was again, and she got a little flutter of panic at the thought of him leaving her on her own. How weird that such a short conversation had shown her what it was like to enjoy a bit of company, even though the subject matter was more than she'd imagined.

He buttered his toast and added a thin layer of jam. She did the same, and they ate quietly, so quietly that she couldn't stand it so got her phone out to play a game.

"What's your name?" he asked.

Oh God, she'd almost said Charlotte then but caught herself in time. She looked up from her screen. "Why, are you going to get your friends to sort me out, shut me up in case I tell the twins something? Like the fact you're staying next door to me?" It was plausible. Gangs did bad shit all the time. She was going to have to make him see she was just some boring old cow who wasn't interested in earning any money from the twins. Not that the money wouldn't be welcome. "Listen, I don't need the hassle, and to be honest, what I don't know won't hurt me, so if you don't blab to me about what you get up to, there's nothing I need to keep quiet, is there?"

He nodded and finished his toast, drank some tea, then stood. "I have to go."

She didn't want him to, but it was obvious he had places to go, people to see. "You know where I am if you fancy a chat later." Fucking hell, could she have sounded more needy?

He nodded. "Thanks for breakfast."

Chapter Twenty-Eight

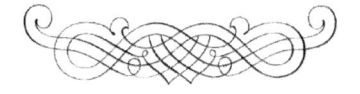

Wednesdays were Sharon's new day off. She'd decided to take more care of herself, to feel better about what she saw when she looked in the mirror. She went to the hairdresser's once a month, had her nails done, and every Wednesday afternoon she walked around the park, getting some steps in. The sun created a golden tint to the leaves and sparkled on the surface of the duck pond, and a welcome breeze sifted through her hair. She carried a large latte in a to-go cup, determined to do ten laps of the park today.

Her phone rang, and she stared at the unknown number on the screen. It could be spam, but it was from a mobile. Probably some call centre. She'd had a really shitty morning, everything that could go wrong had gone wrong, so she was in the mood to have a go at someone, and who better than some prick trying to sell her something she didn't need.

She answered but didn't speak, waiting for an automated voice or the inevitable click where the call had disconnected.

"Sharon?"

"Bloody hell! Maven? Is everything okay?"

"Yeah, we're under the radar. My dad helped us out with finding somewhere to live, getting us new names."

"Thank God. And your mum and sister are okay with relocating? Kingston, wasn't it?"

"Yeah, all good. I just wanted to let you know I'm all right. The twins must have told the UK police about the gang because they've all been rounded up. It hit the news here big time, and my mother put two and two together."

"So she now knows why you had to leave where you used to live?"

"Yeah. What about you? What are you doing?"

She laughed. "It'd take forever for me to tell you everything, but let's just say the issue I had in my past is gone, George and Greg sorted it, and I'm currently walking around the park trying to lose weight. If you ever come back to London, I mean, I don't even know if you can because of getting a passport in your new name and everything, but you'll find me at the Shiny Fork in town."

"I'll Google it. I'd better go. My dad moved with us—not *with* us because my mother wouldn't appreciate that, but he's in Kingston, and we work together on the beach."

"I'm glad everything worked out for you."

"Same. I'll see you."

"Tarra."

Unexpected tears burned her eyes as she slipped her phone in her pocket. In another lifetime things could have been so different. She and Maven…no, there was no point even thinking about it. He lived in Jamaica and she lived here. They weren't meant to be together other than to cross paths so she could help him.

She sipped her coffee and set off at a brisk pace. She had a focus, and that was to be the best version of herself for her sons. They were her life, and she would prove it every day as she slowly packed away pieces of the past, taping up the boxes and stacking them on her mental shelves.

She *could* be a good person, and she was determined to prove it.

Chapter Twenty-Nine

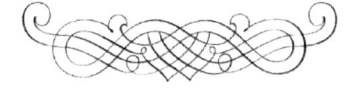

The cobblestone streets seem to twist and turn. Karen raced along, her ankle turning as she stepped down the kerb. The sun had long ago disappeared below the horizon, thank God — there was no way she could do what had to be done in daylight, not like Nathaniel did, and her husband, Henry Greaves, when he'd been in his heyday.

Ahead, long shadows seemed to dance on the ground, eerie undulations that gave her the creeps—as did the idea that people stood in the mouths of darkened alleyways that led to back gardens. In reality, it was likely the birch trees, their leaves swaying in the nighttime breeze.

She kept running, afraid that when she got to her destination she'd be too late. Nathaniel had told her to get there for midnight, and it was quarter past the last time she'd checked her phone.

Almost there.

She put on a burst of speed and rounded the corner, turning into a cobblestone courtyard with a horseshoe of warehouses around the edges. Henry owned them, and they stood in darkness, the windows blank eyes.

Right in the middle lay a body, lifeless, blood spattered on the white shirt. She walked closer, out of breath, angry that she'd missed her chance to be the one to commit this murder. The man on the ground, Paddy Winchester, was known for being a gobby shite who couldn't keep his hands to himself. He sold stuff on the market, shit from the back of a lorry, stuff he nicked from warehouses like these ones.

What had started as an argument in a pub regarding Paddy pinching a woman's arse when he shouldn't have, had now turned into his death. Karen risked switching her phone torch on, lowering the strength of the beam and standing with her back to the road she'd just run in on so if anybody passed by her body would diffuse the glow a bit. His blank stare churned her stomach.

A nearby church clock chimed—it couldn't be one o'clock already, could it? Had she really been standing there for that long? She wasn't sure what she was supposed to do with the body. The plan had been for her to kill Paddy and Nathaniel would do the disposing. There was no contingency for if she didn't make it here. Had he left the body on purpose for her to deal with by herself?

She backed away, losing her footing and stumbling, then she turned to run out of the courtyard. She'd go home. Henry wouldn't even know she'd gone out, he was asleep from the pills she'd put in his whisky earlier.

She darted down narrow pathways, keeping to the shadows as much as possible, panic gripping her at the thought of facing Nathaniel if he was there when she got back.

Would he believe her when she told him why she was late? Probably, but he wouldn't like it. She was his father's wife, so of course she had to have sex with Henry whenever he wanted it—and tonight he had, *before* she'd had a chance to bring him his nightcap.

She neared the house, set in its own grounds, staring into the darkness for some sign of Nathaniel waiting for her, but there was nothing. She crept round the back, entering via the patio doors, and searched the house for him, coming up empty.

Where was he?

She checked in on Henry who slept soundly.

Her phone went off with a message tone, and she quickly went downstairs, sitting on the sofa and gearing herself up to read it.

NATHANIEL: WHERE THE FUCK ARE YOU?

KAREN: WHERE ARE YOU?

NATHANIEL: IN THE WAREHOUSE, LIKE WE SAID.

KAREN: SO YOU DIDN'T DO IT OUTSIDE?

NATHANIEL: WHAT?

KAREN: HE'S ON THE GROUND IN THE COURTYARD. HOW COULD YOU MISS HIM?

Nathaniel: Shit, I didn't put him there.

Karen: Well, it wasn't me! And you're not meant to be texting me!

He didn't respond. She imagined he was going outside to find Paddy, then he'd get rid of the body and clean the blood off the cobbles, so by the time the morning came it would be as if no crime had been committed. But they had a problem on their hands now.

Who had killed Paddy and purposely left him on Greaves' property?

And why?

To be continued in *Resent, The Cardigan Estate 43*

Printed in Dunstable, United Kingdom